KAREN KENDALL

Open Invitation?

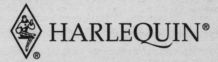

HARLEQUIN®

TORONTO • NEW YORK • LONDON
AMSTERDAM • PARIS • SYDNEY • HAMBURG
STOCKHOLM • ATHENS • TOKYO • MILAN • MADRID
PRAGUE • WARSAW • BUDAPEST • AUCKLAND

ISBN 0-373-79211-5

OPEN INVITATION?

Copyright © 2005 by Karen Moser.

www.eHarlequin.com

Printed in U.S.A.

1

LILIA LONDON, Connecticut etiquette consultant, grimaced as her bra strap fell off her shoulder and down her arm. She shoved it back up—for the third time—and ignored the throbbing of her left big toe, which ached to escape the sling-back she wore.

An etiquette consultant couldn't run around in just her panty hose, and she shouldn't be flashing her lingerie in public, either. Too bad, because the bra was really pretty. Someone besides her should see it....

Lil banished the thought, straightened her posture and edged closer to the eighteenth-century mahogany card table she used as a desk. She peered at her computer.

"In Chinese tradition," she wrote, "the last half of the seventh lunar month is viewed as unlucky for weddings. During this time, the Hungry Ghost Festival is held. It is thought that the gates of Hell are opened, freeing lost spirits to wander the earth. No couple wishes them invited to their nuptials!"

She finished typing the last line of a report on Chinese wedding customs for a client and hit the save button on her computer just as the phone rang.

Now battling an itch in an uncouth place, Lil sighed. It was really tough to be a lady today.

She ignored the itch, crossed her legs and punched the speakerphone button with one tastefully manicured, medium-length nail. "Finesse, Lilia speaking."

"Haaaaaaaaah," said a man's voice, deep and lazy and full of almost sinister sexual vibrations.

Haaaaaaaaaah? Since her mind was more focused on *ni hao,* or hello in Chinese, it took her a moment to process his accent.

"Haaaaaaaaaaah," he repeated. "Maaaah nayme is Dayan Graaanger, Miz Lundun."

My goodness. His Texas drawl was thicker than the peach preserves Nana Lisbeth used to put away each summer.

"Hello, Mr. Granger. How may I help you?"

"I gotch your nayme by way of a Mrs. Shane."

Her partner Shannon's mother. Interesting.

"And the dill is—"

Dill? The spice?

"—I need some emergency, uh, charm school lessons. Mah sister's marryin' some blue-blood Brit and she don't want me to embarrass her at her own weddin'."

Oh, the poor man. So the sister has humiliated him by saying so. Lil's heart went out to him, even though his accent was almost comical. "When will the nuptials take place, Mr. Granger?"

"In two weeks."

Lilia raised an eyebrow and looked at her gilt-edged, blue-leather appointment book. "I'm afraid that I'm out of the office on vacation starting Monday, a week from today. Could you come in tomorrow, perhaps? I think I can clear my afternoon."

"Ahh think this is gonna take more than a single afternoon, Miz London, but I guess I can try to find a flight."

"From where will you be traveling?"

"Amarillo, Texas."

She'd surmised that he was coming from somewhere in the Wild West.

"I can probably give you two and a half days this week, but I'm afraid that's all the time I have," she said regretfully.

"Here's the dill, Miz Granger. Because I'm guilty of procrastinatin' on this, I'm willing to triple your normal fees if you'll take me on. I need dancin' lessons. I need fark lessons. I need—"

Lil paused. *What on earth is a fark?* "Fark lessons, Mr. Granger?"

"You know. Like knife 'n' fark. I've been warned there's gonna be five farks at this damn dinner, and hell if I know what to do with 'em. Also, I need to learn ballroom dancin'—the waltz and that kinda crap. And I need clothes, plus a penguin suit."

Penguin…oh, dear. He needs a great deal more than that, by the sound of it.

"I know it's short notice, Miz London. But I'd make it worth your while. An' I'm a real charmin' guy. It won't be no chore."

Her lips twitched. "Yes, obviously you possess a great deal of ch—ah, charisma, Mr. Granger. But—"

"Ten thousand dollars a week. How does that sound?"

"I beg your pardon?" Lilia blinked rapidly. "I'm not sure I heard you correctly."

"Okay, twelve. But that's my final offer. Twelve thousand a week, for the next two weeks. And I'll pay for your vacation that you have to reschedule, if I'm pleased with your work. A bonus, you could call that."

Lilia's brain didn't require more than a nanosecond to do the math. Twenty-four thousand dollars for Finesse and a free vacation for her? They could hire a PR firm to make a push for more business. And even start anticipating actual salaries!

"Mr. Granger, your offer is very generous." Lil hesitated, torn between wanting her vacation and wanting the business.

"Well, I think so."

She *could* take her vacation a little later. "I do hate to ask, but would you be willing to sign a contract with everything down in black and white?"

"I'll sign my own ass in red permanent marker if you'll take me on."

Lilia tried not to choke. "That—that won't be necessary, Mr. Granger. Why don't you give me your fax number, and I'll send a contract right over?"

"You betcha." He recited the number, and Lilia immediately typed it straight into her computer, where she'd already opened up a file with his name on it. "Mr. Granger? Just for our records, how is it that you know Mrs. Shane?"

"My mother knows her. Some Paris fashion show they both attend? Or some charity event? The kind where you pay five thousand for a plate of rubber veal, soaked in champagne and topped with escargot? The type of thing where everybody there gets to show off their flashy jewels and plastic surgeon's miracles, while feeling smug and righteous 'cuz every sip of their drink costs a hundred bucks."

The man has a chip on his shoulder, that much is certain. Poor guy. It sounds like he really doesn't fit in with his own family. She wondered why he was so different.

Lilia recaptured her thoughts and pressed her lips together, along with her silk hosiery-clad knees. She found something about this man's Texas-accented voice very…carnal.

Which was utterly ridiculous, since she could barely understand that redneck drawl of his. Not to mention the fact that just during their brief conversation so far, he'd butchered the basics of Grammar 101 as she knew it. Still, his voice poured over her like sexual syrup—and she couldn't help liking him.

"Thank you, Mr. Granger," Lilia said. "I look forward to meeting you tomorrow. Will you confirm with me when you find a flight?"

"You betcha."

Lilia smiled. "Goodbye, Mr. Granger."

"Catch ya later, Miz London."

She sat at her desk reflecting for a moment: was it realistic to think she could break his slang speech patterns or change his accent in two weeks? Probably not.

She could dress him and teach him basic table manners, dance steps and polite conversation. She could explain some of the peculiarities of the English language. But as for the rest, no.

She *could* suggest ways of capitalizing on his Texas heritage and demeanor. She could train him to be a charming eccentric: good-humored about his differences. If he was at all good-looking she'd show him how to kiss a lady's hand and compliment her without smarm. The British women would swoon.

However, she was undoubtedly reading too much into that voice. Dan Granger might be gangly, have a prominent Adam's apple and pizzalike skin for all she knew. She'd just have to wait and find out.

Twenty-four thousand dollars for two weeks of work, though! Lilia decided that she didn't care what Dan Granger looked like. She stood up and pirouetted into the reception area. "Shan? Jane? I'm bringing in the big bucks!"

Shannon stuck her blond head out of her office. True to form, she wore tight, black, boot-cut slacks and an electric-blue leather jacket. "Huh? What's this about big bucks?"

"This Texas guy is going to pay us twenty-four thousand dollars to turn him into Pierce Brosnan in two weeks."

Jane stuck her dark, curly head out of her own office. "You're kidding!"

Lil smiled at Jane. She could finally pay her back for bringing her into the business; identifying that she had a unique set of skills that were in demand in the marketplace. Jane had rescued her from a dead-end job as a receptionist in a law firm, and Lil still couldn't believe she was now a professional and a partner in Finesse.

"How raw is the material, Professor Higgins?" Shannon asked, wryly.

Lil's lips twitched and she met their gazes with a steady, even one. "Well…"

"Uh, oh," said Jane.

"I wish you luck," Shannon said.

"Thank you. I think I'll need it, judging by how he handles himself on the phone."

Lilia preferred to work with women. They were easier to mold and they did their homework. Most of the male clients she had were sent by their employers and didn't take etiquette too seriously as a means to move forward in their careers. A mistake, to Lil's thinking.

"So why is this guy paying you so much money?" Jane asked. "Not that I'm complaining."

"Because I'm having to clear my schedule and cancel my vacation in order to complete his transformation in two weeks. His sister is marrying into British aristocracy, and he doesn't want to embarrass her with his crass, crude ways. Incidentally, Shan, we were recommended to him through your mother. She knows *his* mother from either charity events or fashion week."

"Small world. Hey, I guess that means I get a kickback, though, Lil. You can give me a shopping spree at Neiman Marcus." Shannon winked.

"I think not," Lil told her. "Good try, though. You'll have to settle for a PR firm instead."

"Done!" announced Jane.

Shannon frowned. "You're *so* cruel." She wandered into the small kitchenette they all shared. "Hey! Who ate all the crème doughnuts?"

Jane's face was a study in innocence.

"Jane!"

"Who, me?" Then she gave up the pretence. "You ate them all last time!"

"Yes, but that doesn't mean you should descend to my level…"

Jane laughed. Then she turned back to Lilia. "I can't believe you're giving up your vacation in San Francisco for this guy. But thank you."

"It's not a sum I think we should turn down, with the business being so new and all. And besides, he offered to pay for my rescheduled vacation—as a bonus, if he's pleased with my work."

Jane's jaw dropped. "This guy must be either too loaded to care, or truly desperate. He's probably a mess. Are you sure you know what you're getting yourself into?"

Lilia thought about the *farks*. About the *dancin' and crap*. And about the *penguin suit*. She was probably in for a rough time of it.

Was she up to the challenge? "Yes."

Well, it wasn't as if she had a social life lately, since breaking up with her boyfriend of two years after he'd proposed.

She *had* considered marrying Li Wong, a terribly

sweet Chinese man. But the awful truth was more than Shannon's summary of things: that Li's wong was not so long.

He'd wanted Lil to give him a full-body massage every night—without ever returning the favor—learn Cantonese and move to Beijing as his obedient wife.

Lil had very respectfully declined, whereupon Li Wong had informed her that she was ignorant of the great honor he had conferred upon her by even considering a mixed-breed wife. Half American and half Vietnamese? Why, he exclaimed, she wasn't fit to scrub his floors.

That was the moment at which Lilia agreed with his highness: he should leave her disgraceful hovel immediately and never return. So much for Li's beautiful manners and courteous demeanor. Jerk!

She felt a late-afternoon yawn coming on, and delicately covered her mouth with her hand. She'd been through tougher things than this; most recently the loss of her grandmother, who'd raised her. "I'm not afraid of cowboys, Jane. I can handle Dan Granger."

2

A RED-BLOODED AMERICAN guy does not belong in some friggin' charm school.

Dan wiped the sweat from his eyes, neck and naked chest. He stood in faded Wranglers and beat-up ropers at his kitchen sink in Amarillo, Texas, feeling pissed off and reflecting that time ran faster than the water from his faucet.

Lilia London's voice had been like cool water, pouring down the telephone lines. Too bad he hadn't been able to feel it on the back of his neck. Dan grabbed an old hand towel and soaked it under the tap. He wrung it out and pressed it to his face, wiping away some of the day's grime.

Claire can't possibly be getting married. Wasn't his little half sister still a ten-year-old tomboy?

Through the window over the sink, Dan watched two bay quarter horses nip at each other playfully and then swat flies from their flanks with their long black tails.

Beyond their coral, his father stood in paint-spattered overalls with one of the field hands, covering the barn in a fresh coat of deep red. They'd have to scrape and paint the house, next. Dan didn't look forward to the work, but he wouldn't avoid it, either. It was all for a good cause: his dream of starting a boys' retreat out here. Next summer, they'd bring twenty at-risk urban teens out to take classes and work on the ranch. He'd show them a different way of life…and a good time, too.

The interior of the house was sorely in need of a woman's touch, and had been since his mother's departure twenty-two years ago. While Dan wasn't inclined to shop for floral curtains or wallpaper borders, he did see to it that the house was well-maintained on the outside.

Inside they still had the same beat-up plaid sofa they'd had since 1977 and the same worn avocado-green recliner with the ugly crocheted afghan that his aunt Mary Beth had made. Dan had added an area rug he'd had in college, which lent the room a certain something: the smell of old beer.

The walls held nothing but a functional calendar, courtesy of John Deere, and some photos of Dan as a child and his parents. The bridal photograph of his mother in her long white dress was conspicuously absent.

The focal point of the living room was a massive forty-eight-inch wide-screen television, which he'd rather be watching than remembering the conversation he'd had with Mama three weeks ago. It still rankled.

Dan had been scrubbing the dirt out from under his fingernails when the phone rang. The sound was shrill and unrelenting, like a nagging wife. He'd been sorely tempted to ignore it. But with a sigh he'd knocked the faucet to the off position with an elbow and grabbed for the worn dish towel on the countertop. Then he'd picked up the phone and, by doing so, sealed his miserable fate.

"Yo, Granger here."

The connection sounded fuzzy, thousands of miles away, and he didn't need caller ID to know who it was.

Mama…calling from England. He took a deep breath and cracked his neck, his gaze resting again on the stoop-shouldered figure of his father.

"Daniel, really. What kind of greeting is that?" Her voice was peppered with disapproval.

It never ceased to amuse him that the former Louella Granger had trained her West Texas drawl, like some hardy vine, to climb a worldly trellis until it flowered into a British accent.

"It's a functional greetin'," he told her. "Brief, to the point, states who I am. No bullshit about it, Mama."

"Mummy. Please, call me Mummy, dear boy. And don't curse."

Dan grimaced. *Dear boy? Christ. Oh, I say, old chaps. Are y'all fixin' to watch the telly?* "Apologies, Mama. How are you?"

"Splendid! And you?"

"Can't complain. Dad's fine, too, by the way."

She expelled an audible breath.

He added, "Salutations to dear Nigel, of course."

"Daniel, your sarcasm is not appreciated."

"Sarcasm?"

"Nigel is a lovely man. I'm very lucky."

Uh-huh. Nigel-the-Lovely had broken up Dan's parents' marriage without a qualm and whisked Louella off to Merry Olde England without her fourteen-year-old son.

Nigel, being a real peach, hadn't wanted a sullen teenager weighing down the bliss of his new marriage. And Louella had preferred the guilt of leaving her son behind to the realities of raising him. She was very sorry for the way things had turned out, but young Dan had been a little wild and needed the firm guidance that only his father could give him. He was to visit for a month out of every summer though. Wasn't that just divine?

Nope. Dan couldn't stomach tea and crumpets and Lovely Nigel. He'd lasted for exactly ten days on his first visit before announcing that he hated Nigel's stuffy mausoleum, he couldn't stand British food and there was no way in hell he'd ever call Mama "Mummy." He'd taken the first available flight to Dallas. Hard to believe that was twenty-two years ago. Even harder to believe that little Claire, his twenty-one-year-old half sister, was now getting married in just three short weeks. Claire had been the only bright spot in his visits.

Mama waxed poetic and floral about the upcoming wedding, while all he could think about was how he'd adored his little barefoot hellion of a sister. In an odd arrangement, she'd come to visit a few times with Mama.

Claire the sweet, funny tomboy with the sunny personality and Nigel's snooty accent. Dan had taught her to appreciate the value of a good peanut-butter-and-jelly sandwich on Wonder bread instead of those vile crumpets. And as for tea—the only way to drink the stuff, as far as Dan was concerned, was cold and sweet, with a healthy dose of lemon. No fussy porcelain with curlicue handles. No silver sugar tongs. No milk.

"So, darling," his mother said, her voice holding a note of determination. "I said you'd call her. You understand it's only for Claire that I ask."

Huh? He'd obviously missed something. "Mama, I'm sorry—my mind was wandering. Who am I supposed to call?"

"Lilia London, Daniel. Of Finesse."

"And why am I supposed to call this woman?"

"Daniel! I may as well have been talking to a stump. Now listen to me this time."

"Yes, ma'am."

"As I told you, Claire's fiancé is a gentleman of impeccable lineage, and the family is very prominent. His father has a seat in the House of Lords. He's a viscount."

"Yeah, whatever."

"Well, the thing is, Claire wants to be sure the wedding and reception go smoothly. And she doesn't want to…" his mother trailed off delicately. "She would like to avoid embarrassment. Not to mention that she'd like you to be comfortable—"

"I'll be fine. I couldn't care less about rubbing shoulders with the snoots. I'll hang out with the common folk. The, uh, hoi polloi, I believe you call them."

"Yes, well. I'm afraid that there won't *be* any common folk at the festivities, Daniel. That's rather the issue here, darling."

Dan felt irritation spark somewhere in the region of

his liver. Now what? "Would you like me to just stay in the kitchen, then, Mama? Wash the pots and pans?"

"Of course not, silly goose! What a mad idea." She trilled with laughter. "It would never do for the bride's brother to be working in the kitchen."

Of course not. Bad for the family image.

"But you have to admit that you're rather rough around the edges, and this will be a challenging social situation. Five forks at the sit-down dinner, you know. Ballroom dancing with a live orchestra. And a Sunday morning mini-steeplechase—it should have been a hunt, but the horrid government put an end to that—followed by a champagne luncheon."

Dan tried to imagine what in the hell anybody did with five forks at one meal, besides use them to stab obnoxious dinner companions whose politics you didn't agree with.

"…so I want you to call Lilia, dearest. She'll work with you for the next two weeks. Teach you conversation, table etiquette and dancing. She's going to outfit you with proper clothes, too."

The irritation in Dan's liver flamed into full-fledged annoyance, not to mention hurt. "You have got to be kiddin' me. You want to train me like a chimp just for this blasted, stupid, redcoat wedding?"

"It's not blasted and stupid! It's the most important day—weekend—of your sister's life. This is a very small favor to ask."

"Uh-huh. And how much will this small favor cost? Is Lovely Nigel footing the bill?"

Silence. "Daniel, you've done very well for yourself with the ranching and the oil leases. There is no reason Nigel should be asked to…to…pay for your civilization."

Dan stuck a finger in his ear and jiggled it, hard. "My *what?* Did I hear you right? Did you just say my *civilization?*"

Louella sighed. "It's only a figure of speech."

"It's a figure of speech that implies you think I'm a savage!"

"Daniel, on my last visit I distinctly remember you eating some sort of vile pasta product direct from the can with a plastic spoon. You also slept in your clothes."

"I was twenty-two years old! That's how long it's been since you've visited."

"Well, I don't have a great deal of confidence that things have improved much. You may now eat your food from the pot with a fork, that's all."

Dan hated to admit it, but she was right.

"You need some guidance."

"This is insulting. And I gotta point out that *you* are the one who brought me up until *you* left. We never used five forks at *our* dinner table, Mama. One was good enough for you then. Dad and I were good enough for you then. So was Amarillo. But I guess all that has changed."

An awkward silence ensued, and Dan was human enough to savor it. She felt guilty. Well, she should.

Her Southern accent came through more than a little as she said, "Danny, I'm sorry. But I don't know how to fix it now."

There is no fixing it now. But he didn't say it aloud. He stared out at the sparse, dry Amarillo landscape, watching the sun set over the parched grass, scrub and mesquite. Unforgiving, this land was. But so beautiful in a rough, raw way. You couldn't force somebody to appreciate it. They just had to feel it in their bones. And if their bones belonged elsewhere…

Dan sighed. How she could prefer cold and fog and miserable drizzle to the baked heat of Texas, he didn't know. But he supposed she'd done what she had to do: escape. He'd have to forgive her one day.

"Just do it for Claire. Please, Daniel," she said. "Her wedding is very important to her."

"Why didn't she ask me herself?"

"She was too embarrassed. She was afraid to hurt your feelings."

Oh, I see. But you have no worries about that…

"Will you do it, Daniel?" His mother's voice was insistent. She wasn't going to take no for an answer. She'd just keep calling and badger him to death.

Dan sighed. "Who is this woman again?"

"She's the etiquette consultant for a Connecticut-based company called Finesse. They're excellent and come highly recommended. Now write this down."

Dan's mind returned to the present.

For Claire. Not for Mama. It's for Claire that I'm doing this. He was damned if he'd embarrass her at her own wedding. And he didn't know how to fix himself to her satisfaction.

Dan rubbed a weary hand across the slight fur of his

chest when he hung up. He stared at the name and number he'd scrawled. Lilia London. What a priss-pot, pretentious name. He'd bet it was made up, like a stage name, to fit her profession.

He imagined himself calling her. *Well, Martha Stewart was in jail, so I contacted you...*

Claire's request hurt. He'd never ask *her* to change one bit...but all the indicators pointed to the fact that she had. She'd become the sort of person who cared about forks and steeplechases and image. Well, tally friggin' ho. He was off to Farmington, Connecticut.

DESPITE HER SNOTTY NAME, Dan entertained himself on the long flight by trying to imagine what Lilia London looked like.

Her voice was cool, elegant and pure. Like the finest vodka poured neat—straight from the freezer. It was the voice of a 1950's movie star: an untouchable, impeccable but oh-so-sexy Audrey Hepburn. Audrey in sterling silver garters.

Dan couldn't get Lilia's crisp enunciation and continental accent out of his baked Texas brain. Truth to tell, her voice did strange and embarrassing things to him. His soldier had come right to attention; a missile at the ready, locking on target. The soldier eagerly anticipated five farks, but not the kind you set next to a dinner plate.

Dan told him to stand down. And at ease. Because though Lilia London's voice still echoed in his head, she was over a thousand miles away and he didn't even know what she looked like. She could be the size of a redwood tree, with a beard and manly hands. But somehow he didn't think so. He had a feeling that her voice was bigger than she was. She'd be petite and porcelain, the kind of girl who got caught in a dapper hero's fierce embrace by the end of an old film. The closed-mouth kiss was passionate enough to rattle her pearls, but Metro Goldwyn Meyer soon faded her to black, fully clothed.

The Audreys of the world wouldn't know what to do in contemporary Hollywood. Dan tried and failed to imagine her in current love scenes. They would ruin her mystique. Tarnish the whole concept of a lady.

Dan closed his eyes and drifted off into a light, fitful sleep. He kept seeing a ten-year-old Claire walking down the aisle of a church, wearing jeans with holes in the knees. She got to the end and took the hand of a pompous ass in tails and a top hat. The kind of guy the English would refer to as a real "prat." Ugh.

Dan awoke as the jet landed with a bump. The roar of brakes filled his ears while the flight attendants commanded everyone to stay seated until the captain had turned off the seat belt sign. They hoped he'd enjoyed his flight, had a pleasant stay at his final destination and would think of their airline again next time he traveled.

Yeah, yeah, yeah. Dan pulled his overnight bag out of the overhead compartment, helped an older woman with hers and waited with the rest of the herd to get off the plane.

A walk through the terminal and a rental car later, he emerged from Bradley Airport's roundabout and onto the highway. He was a forty minute drive from his destination of Farmington, Connecticut, home of the legendary Miss Porter's preparatory school for young women. Maybe Farmington was chock full of Audrey Hepburns. It wasn't such a horrible vista to contemplate, since she was a hot little babe.

If only he could meet the Audreys without taking classes in some friggin' charm school.

LILIA LOOKED UP from her computer as the glass door of Finesse opened with a bit of a crash and something dropped to the floor with a thud. She left her delicate reading glasses on her nose as she got up and walked to the door of her office.

"Howdy!" said a tall, tanned, younger version of the Marlboro Man. He wore Western boots. He sported a belt buckle the size of a satellite dish, affixed to a hand-tooled leather belt that she was terribly afraid had his name etched into the back—the distressing equivalent of a dog collar, as far as she was concerned. And worse, far worse, he actually wore a Stetson on his head. The two-day stubble she could live with, since it was in vogue and somewhat George Clooneyish. The scarred, weathered hands might be a problem in his transformation. But his posture was good—excellent for such a tall man.

And the bulge in his pants was quite impressive…. Shocked at herself for even letting her eyes wander there, Lilia blushed. She ended her quick inventory with a gracious hello.

"Are you Miz London?"

"I am. And you must be Mr. Granger. How are you?" Lil extended her hand.

He stuck out a big paw and shook it. "Cain't complain."

He had the warmest, firmest handshake she'd ever encountered. It almost dislodged her arm from the socket, though. He was roughly twice her size. "Pleasant flight?"

"The usual. Microscopic packets o' trail mix and a weak soft drink over too much ice. Lots of orders to fasten my seat belt and enjoy the ride." Granger grinned down at her, seeming unwilling to relinquish her hand. He looked deeply and frankly into her eyes and she felt something inside her melting.

She slowly disentangled her hand, unable to look away from his sardonic and wildly sexy mouth. Rimmed by unshaven stubble, his lips sat cockily over a cleft chin set in a strong, angular jaw.

"Aw, do I have to give that back, Miz London?" He was referring to her hand. "I thought maybe it was mine to keep."

Again, she fell into that smile, even though it was a cheesy line. This cowboy was something else. Her heart did a slow roll in her chest, and she blinked.

The man may not have manners, but he does have magnetism—even if it's all animal. "Nice compliment," she said, by way of recovery. "Very good. We can work with that." She nodded and smiled like a benevolent professor.

Granger shoved his own hands into his pockets and rocked back on his heels as he looked down at her. His mouth twisted. "Thank you, ma'am. If I had a tail, I'd wag it for ya, in hopes of gettin' a Scooby snack."

Lilia tilted her head and evaluated him. Not stupid, in spite of the twang and the slang. He knew when he was being patronized. She'd have to be careful. "Why don't we go into my office," she suggested. "Would you like a cup of coffee?"

"Don't mind if I do."

"Cream? Sugar?"

"Just hot 'n' black."

She restrained herself from adding the words "please" and "thank you" for him, walked to the antique mahogany desk that had been her grandmother's and retrieved a neatly prepared file. "While I get that for you, you may want to have a look at our contract."

"All right. Uh, d'you have somewhere I can put my hat?"

"Of course," Lilia said automatically, and found herself holding the Stetson without the faintest idea what to do with it. She cast a glance at the bronze bust of her grandfather Henry London, who had been knighted by the Queen of England for distinguished work in the sciences.

Sir Henry sat on a pedestal in a corner of her office. He was terribly dignified and wore a bow tie. A wicked impulse took hold of her. For the next couple of hours, he could also wear a cowboy hat. She took it over to him and perched it on his head at a jaunty angle.

Granger grinned. "Gives the old pompous ass a little personality, don't it?"

Lilia froze. With silent apologies to Grandfather

Henry, she aimed a genteel smile in the cowpoke's direction and said nothing. It would be rude to embarrass him, no matter how tempting. She handed him the file.

Granger took the file and sprawled into her visitor's chair, denim-covered knees spread wide. He began to whistle while reading. He cracked his knuckles.

Oh, dear. Lilia didn't slap herself in the forehead for taking on this handsome yokel, but maybe she should have. Could she really transform him?

She made a beeline for the kitchenette to get his coffee. She poured a cup for him and one for herself, using her grandmother's Royal Doulton china: very thin, very old, hand-painted.

She sang softly as she set a tray with the cups, saucers, cream, sugar and linen napkins. She added a plate of artistically arranged cookies and fresh strawberries and two silver spoons, also her grandmother's. Nana Lisbeth's third commandment was: *Food should always look pretty. It tastes better that way.*

With perfect posture, Lilia lifted the tray and glided toward her office, ignoring Shannon who winked at her and lifted her Diet Coke can in a parody of English manners, waving her pinky finger in an exaggerated fashion. Shan's hideous rendition of "God Save the Queen" did make Lil laugh, though.

She swept into her office with a smile still on her face, though she felt it wobble when she beheld Dan Granger's booted foot propped against the edge of her desk.

"What exotic-looking boots you're wearing, Mr. Granger!" she exclaimed, hoping he'd take the hint.

"Elephant hide," he nodded. "Check 'em out." He slid the boot farther onto her desk for her perusal. "Cost me a damn arm and a leg, but well worth it."

She kept her smile fixed in place as she moved around the other side of the desk and placed the tray squarely in the middle of it. "I do hope the elephant agrees with you."

Dan guffawed and didn't move his boot in spite of the proximity of the food.

Lilia squinted meaningfully at it, but he must have been convinced that she was admiring the awful footwear. She slid the tray closer to the boot, and then closer, until she actually nudged it and he took the hint. "Your coffee, Mr. Granger."

He eyed the beautifully set tray uneasily. "The Sunday china, huh? I'm honored."

"No, no. I use this every day. Here you are," she said as she handed him his cup and saucer. He needed to get comfortable with this sort of thing.

His big paws dwarfed the delicate bone china and he looked at it as if it might bite. "I'm awful afraid I might drop this."

"Of course you won't," she said with loads of cheer.

He lifted the cup by its tiny, finely crafted handle, which disappeared entirely behind his big fingers. He took a slurp and then gingerly set cup and saucer down on the corner of her desk, watching as she prepared her own coffee.

"Would you like a cookie? A strawberry?" She held the plate out to him. Granger snagged a cookie and popped the whole thing into his mouth while she watched, horrified and yet fascinated by the clean, no-nonsense appetite of the gesture.

She had to admire the even white teeth crunching down on the cookie, devouring it in a single bite. And the nod and grin of simple appreciation as he said, "Mmm. That's *good.*"

She also couldn't help but notice the heavily muscled, tanned arm that helped perform the gesture. In fact, his bicep was quite delicious. She nibbled delicately on her own cookie. *And look, there's a matching bicep right over there. Plus an intriguing, broad expanse of chest under the snug T-shirt, a flat belly underneath and...oh, dear.* She was looking there again.

How could she? But just that tiny peek had revealed a...well, she really shouldn't have noticed, but...*it*... went quite a distance down his right thigh from where *it* originated.

"Miz London? Your file?"

She blinked. He'd extended her manila folder to her, across the desk. "Oh, yes, of course. Excuse me." She put out her hand to take it, her cheeks heating, and fixated on that sexy mouth and chin again. Suddenly an image of them *right between her legs* shocked her and she reared back, dropping the file. What in heaven's name was wrong with her?

The papers hit the floor in a messy cascade, and she reached down for them at the same time he did, their faces almost colliding. "Excuse me!" she said.

"Pardon me," he said. He straightened and took a step

back, hip jogging the corner of the desk and then, most unfortunately, the Royal Doulton cup and saucer. They crashed to the floor and splintered while black coffee splashed onto her hand-embroidered cream rug.

"Oh! Oh, oh!" Lil repeated stupidly, staring at the mess.

"Dad gummit!" exclaimed Granger, his expression appalled. Then he peeled off his T-shirt.

"What! *What are you*—"

He dropped it onto her carpet and placed his boot on it, mopping up the excess coffee while she sputtered and stared at his naked, furred chest and flushed bright red and then sputtered some more. "No! Thank you. Don't rub! *Blot*." she finally managed to get out. Then Lil ran for the kitchenette and club soda and carpet cleaner.

Jane was there, peering into the refrigerator with a hopeful expression. "What's the matter?"

"Spill," Lil said. "Destroyed Royal Doulton, Nana Lisbeth's. And he's half-naked in my office! Give me the club soda, please."

Jane looked at her as if she were an escaped lunatic. "Half naked in your office? Cow patty man?"

Lil nodded and rushed off with the soda, the carpet cleaner, a dish towel and the dustpan. Not surprisingly, Jane followed, unable to resist.

Dear God, the man's back…a beautiful, bronzed jigsaw of perfectly placed muscle, moving with sinuous grace as he blotted her carpet with his own T-shirt—the savage. The sweet, helpful, magnificent barbarian. In that ridiculous leather belt with D-A-N carved into the back of it.

Despite the idiotic belt and the fact that he'd destroyed Nana Lisbeth's china, a hot electric flash drove through Lil's core. Part of her wanted to grab him by the belt buckle that ate Dallas and pull off his pants, too. She ignored the renegade impulse. It wasn't at *all* ladylike.

"Thank you, Mr. Granger," she said firmly, taking over. "Really, you didn't have to use your shirt for cleanup."

He moved aside and shrugged. "I got ten more in my carry-on bag. No big deal. I do apologize for bustin' your dishes. I really, really do. Can I buy you a new set? I know how you women are about matched sets of things."

You can't replace a sentimental, family piece. Lil poured club soda over the soiled area of the rug. "No, no, of course not. These things happen. You're very sweet to offer, though." She forced herself to smile at him, set him at ease again, minimize his embarrassment and guilt. That was the polite thing to do.

But it was a bad idea, since she couldn't seem to look away from his pectorals and that quite stunning abdomen and…*no*. She would *not* look lower again. *There are some packages that are not meant to be opened.*

As she blotted up the stain, he must have noticed Jane in the doorway. "Haaaaaaaaaaaaaa."

"Hi," Jane said, a tremor of amusement in her voice.

"Dan Granger, ma'am. Klutz at large."

"Jane O'Toole. You're obviously not from around here."

"Amarillo, darlin'. Pardon me while I grab another shirt from my bag."

"Oh, feel free," Jane said.

Lil and Jane both watched as he rummaged through a beat-up canvas duffel next to two large suitcases—Lil had told him to bring anything he planned on taking to London—and pulled out a spare shirt. They continued to watch as, oblivious, he raised his arms with a ripple of muscle and then stuck his head through the neck hole, with yet another ripple. Lilia's mouth went dry and she found herself on the receiving end of an infuriating smirk from Jane. "Nice to meet you, Dan," she said. "I've got to get back to work." And with a knowing grin in Lil's direction she did so.

Well, that settled it. Even if Granger spoke proper English, was the last virile man on the planet, and her life depended upon it, Lil would never "go there." Because Jane wouldn't ever let her live it down.

Granger was now digging deep into the pocket of his Wranglers, which only served to pull the fabric hard against his—that, uh, most interesting bulge. Lil pressed her lips together. She knelt down and concentrated on sweeping the shards of Nana Lisbeth's cup and saucer into the dustpan.

"Here," said Granger's voice. "I'd really feel better if you'd take this."

She looked up, straight into his crotch and dropped the dustpan. The shards scattered again. He held out a wad of green bills.

Soft laughter came from the hallway and she saw Shannon disappearing into the kitchenette. Lil had to admit that she and Granger must make an interesting vignette: she on her knees in front of him, while he held out a wad of cash.

"Mr. Granger, I couldn't possibly—"

"Dan," he said. "Just call me Dan, honey."

That was another thing they needed to address: he couldn't walk around calling every female he met "sweetheart," "darlin'," or "honey." "Mr. Granger, I know that things are different down south, but—"

"Dan," he repeated, squatting down with her and gently taking the dustpan from her hands. They spoke at the same time.

"—you mustn't use terms of endearment with women you don't know, as you risk—"

"Don't worry, in London I'll call the ladies 'love.'"

"—offending them."

They squatted on her rug, knee to knee and face-to-face. She could see the pores in his skin, the tiny lines on his lips, the intense, hungry look in his eyes.

He swept the shards back into the dustpan. "Besides bustin' your china and trashing your rug," he drawled, "do I offend you, Lilia?"

She opened her mouth to say yes. Then no. Then yes.

His blue gaze engulfed her, spread over her skin like the soft sting of an astringent; cool and hot at the same time. After a moment, he reached out an index finger and stroked along her jaw to just under her chin. He tilted it up and angled his face over hers while her heart galloped around in her chest like a mad thing. He was much, much too close to her.

She was much, much too close to him.

And she didn't want to do a damn thing about it.

SHE'S AN EXOTIC porcelain doll. Perfect, delicate features. Dark eyes full of foreign ritual and pageantry. Lips that whispered of mystery and private pleasures.

She's the kind of woman who was born on a pedestal, though. An untouchable Audrey, full of silver screen mystique. A china figurine with a painted-on skirt that no man ever got beneath.

A damn shame. Dan would like to see what Lil's hair looked like tumbled around her face and neck, instead of in that sleek style she wore. He'd like to see that prim blouse of hers unbuttoned, skimming just over what he imagined were small, pink nipples. He'd love to see her barefoot, with her skirt hiked up to a point just shy of indecency.

And if he didn't stop his thoughts from wandering down this path, he was going to embarrass himself. He hadn't missed the self-conscious flush on her cheeks at their former position: him handing her money while she balanced on her knees in front of him.

And seeing how prim and proper she was, how utterly alien that position probably was to her, turned him on even more. He'd also seen her glance at places she shouldn't, which sent quick lust spiraling through him. He wanted to get primal with this exotic little Audrey; see if Miss Manners knew what to do with a real man.

Of course, smashing a woman's good china was generally not the way into her bed. That had been a real smooth move.

He'd seen the sudden flash of anguish when the cup hit the floor, even if she'd quickly disguised it. He felt like a shit-heel.

Were you born in a barn? Mama had yelled at him once.

I don't know, Mama, you tell me. A rude response, one that did him no honor. But one that channeled his anger at her and her disappearance and her social climbing.

He still couldn't believe he was here at friggin' *charm school*. Dan reminded himself that he was doing this for Claire, and Claire alone.

And regarding this weird attraction to Lilia London? He'd taken Psych 101 in college. That old goat Freud would probably explain it as a rebel, subconscious urge. Was his lust for the china doll an instinct to literally screw manners? Yep. That's all it was. Dan was sure of it.

3

LILIA RETURNED to her senses and backed away from the animal and his magnetism before he got any closer and...and...kissed her or something. God forbid.

Because kissing clients was not acceptable. And judging from this man's awful performance in her office just now, she needed to get right to work on him.

She sat in her Queen Anne chair and demurely crossed her feet at the ankles, knees together. She clasped her hands in her lap and smiled while Dan made himself comfortable—or tried to—in her visitor's seat. He dwarfed the antique, and she heard an ominous creak as he tried to lounge against the back of it.

Dan froze, hearing it, too. He shot her an uneasy glance. "This thing gonna hold up under my weight?"

"It should be fine," Lilia told him, praying that this was indeed so. Like most of the pieces in her office, the chair had belonged to Nana Lisbeth, who hadn't believed in reproductions. She'd been terribly old-school and formal.

Dan spread his knees, ready to frog-leap out of the chair at a moment's notice. She hid a smile.

"Shall we get right to work, then?"

"Why not."

"Fine. Then let's begin by going over your, ah, performance since you arrived."

"My performance?" Dan seemed taken aback.

"Your…behavior. And ways in which it can improve."

He shrugged and then nodded.

"Now, for starters, let me say that the correct way to behave is almost always what makes the people around you comfortable. I'm probably about to make you rather *un*comfortable, but it's in the spirit of learning, all right? And I apologize beforehand."

"All righty."

"Let's talk about greetings. When you came in, I believe you said, 'howdy.' Is that correct?"

"Yup."

"Let's change that to merely 'hello.' And 'yup' to 'yes.' Then there's the issue of your Western hat. That absolutely must come off before you enter a building." *In fact, it should be left behind in Texas or burned.*

"I'm sorry, ma'am, I did know that. I just lost my manners when I saw how gosh-darned pretty you are."

Lil flushed. "Thank you. But that leads us into another issue. Your compliments are charming, but for Connecticut or England, they may be a bit effusive."

"E-what?"

"Florid." Seeing him look more confused than ever, she added, "Too much. Over the top."

"I can't tell a woman she's pretty?"

"You can, but perhaps in a less familiar way. Now, when I offered you coffee, you said—"

"Don't mind if I do."

"Yes, please," Lilia corrected. "And you always say 'thank you' when a beverage is given to you."

"Okay."

"When I offered you the plate of cookies and fruit, you put an entire cookie into your mouth. That's not acceptable. You need to make it last at least three bites, and of course you'll never talk with your mouth full."

"No, never," he said solemnly.

"Now, let's talk about your boots. While they are indeed very fine, they never, under any circumstances, belong on a desk or any other kind of furniture."

He muttered an apology and looked slightly shame-faced.

Lilia forged ahead. "Breaking the cup and saucer was an accident, and it could have happened to anyone. However, you should never again disrobe in a place of business."

"I was trying to save your rug!" he exclaimed.

"I do realize that, and I thank you. However, a paper towel would have sufficed."

"You ladies sure didn't seem to mind the view."

She blinked rapidly. "Regardless, no public shirt removal. Is that clear?"

"Yes, mistress."

No mistaking the mockery in his voice. She glanced sharply at him. "You find this amusing, Mr. Granger?"

"Yes, ma'am, I do."

"It's really no laughing matter."

"Sorry, Miz London, but I can laugh at just about anything. It's a fault of mine." His hazel eyes danced.

As faults went, she supposed that one wasn't too awful. One needed a sense of humor to survive in this world.

Lil studied his face, which was framed by short, wavy, chestnut hair—the same color as the sprinkling of it she'd seen on his bare torso. She had the oddest desire to tangle her fingers in it, rake them over his bare skin, burn her cheeks against the bristle on his own.

The man had a most disturbing effect upon her. She'd never wanted to rub herself shamelessly against Li Wong, or run her fingers through *his* chest hair. Probably because he'd had a total of three chest hairs, and was otherwise bald as a baby's…

"I wasn't laughing at you, Miz London. Just at your, uh, dedication to your job. And the fear on your face as you realized just how raw your material was."

Lil raised an eyebrow. "The boots on my desk were a bit much. Even you know better than that. You were testing me."

"Maybe," he admitted.

"I may be small, Mr. Granger, but I'm not stupid or fainthearted. I'm not afraid to take you on."

He grinned and openly evaluated her body. "You *are* tiny," he said. "What size are you? Do they make a size that small?"

"Never, ever, ask a woman her dress size or her age, Mr. Granger. Or her true hair color. Those are not socially acceptable questions."

"What if you're just asking in order to buy her a gift?"

"You make an educated guess. If the item doesn't fit, she'll exchange or return it. But a gift of clothing really isn't proper. Jewelry, yes. A scarf, a silver compact, chocolates or perfume—all perfectly acceptable."

"How 'bout lingerie?"

"Out of the question, unless—" Lil felt heat warming her cheeks "—you've been, ah, intimate for quite some time."

He looked at her boldly. "Intimate, huh?"

Impossible, but Lil could actually feel his gaze undressing her…unbuttoning her blouse, unhooking her bra, pushing up her skirt and discovering that she wore no panties under her stockings, because she couldn't stand thongs but considered panty lines utterly unacceptable.

Heat bloomed between her thighs, shocking her, and she pressed her knees even more firmly together.

"Mr. Granger, as long as we're on the topic—which isn't socially acceptable, either, by the way—"

"You brought it up." He grinned that shameless grin of his.

To her horror, she realized that she had indeed brought it up…and not only the topic. Where was her self-control? She'd looked at him *there* again, and Granger's package had, ah, supersized, in fast food parlance.

She swallowed.

His lips twitched. He didn't appear to care! He swung one booted foot over another, crossing his legs.

Thank you, God. "As I was saying, it's not proper for you to…openly evaluate a woman like that."

"Like what?" he asked softly, a devilish smile now playing over his lips.

"You know exactly what I mean. You weren't discreet in the least."

"Is it proper, Miz London, to stare at a man's equipment while he's in your visitor's chair?"

She opened her mouth as fire rushed along her cheeks. She shut it again. She searched for the breath his words had knocked out of her body. Finally she was able to speak. "I did no such thing, Mr. Granger."

"Is that what you call a little white lie, Miz London? Because I call it a big ol' fib."

"Mr. Granger!"

"Ma'am?"

She took a deep breath and steepled her fingers on her desk. "Even if I were lying, which I assure you that I am not, it is not socially correct to call me on the lie. Conversation should be smooth, and one steers away from topics which could be…"

"Sticky?"

Her nostrils flared and she did her very best not to glare at the man. "Difficult."

Apparently he decided to give her a respite, for he asked about the framed pictures on her wall. "Who's the older couple?"

"My grandparents, Sir Henry and Lisbeth London. He was British. She's American. They met during World War II."

"Sir Henry?"

"Yes. He was knighted by the queen for distinguished

work in the sciences—meaning that he discovered a preservative for tinned meat. Not terribly glamorous, but useful." She smiled.

"No sh—uh, kidding! He musta made a killing off that."

"Mr. Granger, it's not at all polite to comment about someone's financial status—especially not face-to-face."

"All I said was—"

"It can be construed as fishing for information."

"Well, don't *construe* it that way, because I didn't mean—and why can't you say 'take'? Nice, plain English." He shook his head.

Lilia tightened her lips. "One, when words have left your mouth, you have no control over how they are taken. Two, what isn't plain English about the word 'construe'? And three, Sir Henry didn't file a patent in time, so he never made much off his preservative, sad to say. Which is why I have a job."

He folded his arms across his broad chest and uncrossed his long legs. His boot began to tap on the floor. "You're very formal, Miz London."

"I'm an etiquette consultant, Mr. Granger. And I'm sorry if I'm annoying you, but you did come to me for guidance." She gazed at him steadily.

He didn't growl, but he looked as if he wanted to. "Tell me about the younger couple in the other frame. The Asian lady and the officer."

She nodded. "My parents, Lieutenant Bryce and Su Yi London. They met while my father was stationed in Vietnam. He finished his first tour, then brought her home as his bride. They had six months together before he was called for a second tour. He didn't return."

"I'm real sorry to hear that."

"Thank you."

"And your mother? Does she still live in the States?"

"No. She died of a rare blood disorder when I was small. My grandmother raised me." *This conversation is getting too personal.* "More coffee, Mr. Granger?"

"Again, I'm sorry—uh, no thank you."

"A cookie? A strawberry?" She held out the tray to him. He selected a butter cookie and two large strawberries, putting them on his plate.

He picked up a strawberry, cast a sidelong glance at her, and asked, "I don't have to eat this with a fark or somethin', do I?"

He looked so boyish and uncertain that she chuckled. "No. You may grasp it by the stem and eat it—preferably in more than one bite." She demonstrated by taking a small bite of her own strawberry.

He brought the fruit to his lips and touched his tongue to it, rubbing the tip over the strawberry's texture. Then his even, white teeth sank into it, slicing through the delicate flesh and taking it for his own.

Lilia clamped her knees together yet again as a hot, unwelcome twinge occurred between her thighs.

Granger licked juice from his bottom lip and devoured the rest of the strawberry while she secretly envied it and squirmed discreetly in her chair. Heaven help her if she sprouted a little green stem and matching jester's collar.

He tilted his head. "Are you feeling all right, Miz London?"

"Why, I'm just fine, thank you."

"You sure? You look kinda like you have gas. Did you have a lot of these strawberries for breakfast or something?"

Lilia didn't know whether to laugh or cry. "Mr. Granger! That isn't a socially acceptable thing to say, either. You must never, ever tell a lady that she looks as if she has indigestion."

"Why not just plain gas?"

"It's not at all polite! Never, ever mention bodily functions or discomforts of that nature—that's simply appalling manners."

"You think I'm appalling?" asked her horrifying new client, holding out an open package of Rolaids.

She shook her head. "No, thank you, Mr. Granger. I don't require one of those—"

"Well, I always take two. Used to have the constitution of a goat until I hit my thirties, but now…not that I was implying that you're, uh, aging or anything." He stopped, seeming to realize that he was only digging himself in deeper. Then he began to laugh.

She stared at him in disbelief, fighting the urge to bang her forehead against the polished surface of the eighteenth-century card table.

"I guess that wasn't too smooth, was it?"

"Correct."

"So you do think I'm appalling. That's okay, my

mother does, too. That's why I'm here. Do I have to go sit in the corner, wearing the social dunce cap, now?"

Lil took a deep breath. "Of course I don't find you appalling. Your manners do, ah, need some work. But instead of sitting here and correcting you all day, I think it might be beneficial for you to watch some Cary Grant films. That is the general demeanor we're aiming for, with you. We'll take you from crude cowboy to gentleman rancher. His civilized persona is perfect."

"So right now I'm *un*civilized." He winked at her.

"I didn't say that. You're a bit of a rogue, that's all."

"Oh, I like that. Rogue is real nice and old-fashioned. Makes me want to grow a handlebar mustache and, you know, swashbuckle a little. Is swashbuckle a verb, Miz London? And if so, how do ya do it?"

"I don't have the faintest idea," Lil said, a laugh escaping her at the ridiculous concept.

"To swashbuckle, or not to swashbuckle, that is the question…" Granger threw his arms wide and leaned back dramatically in her visitor's chair.

The ominous creak of before became a loud crack, and the Queen Anne disintegrated under his weight.

Speechless, Lilia jumped up, her hand over her mouth.

On his back, her client peered at her from between his airborn western boots. "You know," he said, "I do believe it might be bad manners to seat your guests on ancient, decrepit furniture."

"Are you all right?" she asked. She extended her hand to help him up.

"Well, I still don't have a clue what to 'swash' means, but I seem to have buckled the chair."

"Perhaps it's the masculine of 'swish'? Lil suggested.

Granger laughed. Then he took her hand and got up. He continued to hold it as they both surveyed the remnants of the chair in silence.

"I'm real sorry," he said.

"I do apologize," she said at the same time.

A long, pregnant pause followed.

"That's all right. I'm sure it would be impolite for me to sue you for damages." He grinned to soften his words.

Lil drew her eyebrows together and tried to tug her hand from his, but he held on. Very unladylike and disconcerting sexual charges zipped from her hand to other parts of her body. Unmentionable ones.

"Tell you what," he said, bending his head close to hers.

She swallowed, feeling dwarfed by his big body and mesmerized by his eyes. "What?"

"I won't sue you if you'll give me a kiss."

4

REAL SMOOTH, DAN. You smash the woman's chair, make an ass out of yourself, mock her and threaten her. Now you're trying to blackmail her and kiss her, too? What in the hell is wrong with you, man?

But he still held her tiny, fine-boned hand captive in his, while she stared at him with those unbelievably hot, smoldering black eyes of hers. They were exotic, beautifully shaped and slanted down at the outside corners. They were framed by long, sooty lashes that, at the moment, stabbed upward like tiny black daggers toward his face.

"You've got a nerve, Mr. Granger," she said. But her hand trembled in his and her lips—pale, perfect, prim—parted ever so slightly.

It was all the opening Dan needed. He angled his face over hers, inhaled her fragrance of jasmine and sweet floral soap, and ever-so-gently touched the tip of his tongue to her pale lips.

Hers parted even more, surprised. He continued to taste her in tiny degrees, taking in the fresh strawberry essence on those lips, the faint traces of Ceylon tea, the sweetness of butter-cookies.

Since she made no move of protest, he settled his lips on hers and kissed her hungrily, dominating her mouth with his own. She opened at his insistence and he explored her, feeling the smooth surfaces of her teeth, nipping at the plumpness of her bottom lip, and rubbing languorously against the tip of her tongue with his own.

She made a faint, ladylike noise of either submission or approval, and it drove him wild.

He wanted to see her naked skin, feel the flesh of her thigh, lick the curve of her breast. Tongue her nipple, hear her moan into his ear, plunge a finger inside her.

Dan wanted to penetrate that Audrey Hepburn coolness and take her from the gates of proper to the open field of thrashingly, screamingly *im*proper.

He was scant inches away from closing his hand over her breast when some internal monitor in his brain informed him that it would be a very, very bad idea.

Lilia wasn't a woman he could push into sex. He had to make her want it as badly as he did. He had to tease her until she couldn't help herself.

He didn't know how he knew it, but he did. One wrong move, and he was toast. He pulled away from her and searched for her reaction.

She refused to look him in the eye, but her breathing was fast and uneven, just the way he'd hoped. After a moment she said, "I can't believe you just did that, Mr. Granger." And she smoothed an invisible wrinkle out of her immaculate skirt.

"Neither can I. But since I did, do you think you

could call me Dan? And maybe, just maybe, I could call you Lilia?"

"I suppose that would be acceptable, now that you're not going to sue me."

"I was kidding about that."

"I know."

"But you kissed me anyway?"

She tucked her dark hair behind her ears and blushed. "Well, I felt guilty about the chair."

Dan put his tongue into his cheek and shoved his hands into his pockets. "You sure know how to flatter a guy."

She dimpled, flashed her gaze upward to his, and then bent to pick up the broken chair. He should have helped her, but he stood mesmerized by the way her skirt pulled across her sweet little hips and highlighted the curves of the most perfect derriere he'd ever seen. It was a shameful waste that she sat on that, and covered it with suits, because it rivaled any ass he'd ever seen twirling around a pole. But it was the untouchable quality of it that mesmerized him.

There wasn't a panty line on it, either, and Dan's mouth went dry wondering if that meant what he thought it did.

Miss Manners, commando? Bare to the air? *Oh, get a grip, Granger.*

Unfortunately that was precisely what he wanted to do: get a good grip. Each of her little cheeks would fit nicely in the palm of his hand. He'd squeeze. He'd stroke. He'd caress and then trail his fingertips inward to brush her intimate folds.

Granger. Do you need to buy the latest issue of Play-boy *and lock yourself in a bathroom? Christ!*

"I, uh. I can try to fix that for you," he said, gesturing at the chair.

"That's all right. I'll take it to a furniture-maker. Are you sure you didn't hurt your back? Your tailbone?"

"I'm fine. I've fallen off a lot of horses, and they tend to be taller than your average dining room chair. Plus a chair don't drag you by a stirrup or kick you in the head on its way back to the barn."

"Very true," agreed Lilia. "They smell better, too."

"You don't like the smell of a good, sweaty horse? Mmmm. I love it. Raw and salty and musky. Pungent. Laced with saddle-leather and liniment." *The only smell that comes close is…sex.* But he didn't say it aloud. That might send Miss Manners right over the edge.

She was already staring at him as if he had three heads. "Dan, if you think horses smell good, may I enquire as to what you think smells bad?"

He thought for a second. "Those candle shops, the ones where the fakey-fruit and sickly cinnamon and vomit-vanilla scents all combine to blow the hair right off your head when you walk in the door. Now those places stink to high heaven. I'd rather shovel out a horse stall any day than have to spend two minutes in a place like that."

Lilia laughed.

He loved it when she laughed: the sound was simultaneously throaty and musical. Her pointed little chin rose, her sleek black hair a shiny curtain along her smooth, pale neck.

Then there were the eyebrows. Lilia London had the most flawlessly groomed, dark, winged eyebrows he'd ever seen. They added to her untouchable look, yet also projected exoticism and a challenging sexuality.

He was curious about her reaction to the kiss. He'd expected her to be flustered by it, shocked, uncomfortable in his presence afterward. Frankly he'd thought that it would put an end to their session today. But it had been a risk he took willingly, just for a taste of her.

"You're an unusual man, Dan," she said. "Now, we have a lot to do in two weeks, so let's set up a schedule. We should start analyzing your wardrobe and replacing items today. My partner Shannon is an image consultant and she will help with that. She'll take your measurements, get your shoe size and go off shopping on her own. We'll get a tailor in here to fit everything perfectly. But I want to take you to be fitted for at least one custom suit and, of course, your evening wear. That cannot be off-the-rack for this particular wedding.

"I'm going to strongly suggest that you leave your boots, hat and belt…" her voice trailed off as she stared at it, "behind. Under no circumstances should they go to London with you."

"Whoa. My boots are the most comfortable footwear I own. In Texas you wear 'em with a suit. I've even seen them worn with a tux."

Lilia closed her eyes and visibly shuddered. "Never, *ever* wear boots with a suit of any kind. Please. Especially not outside of your home state. You will be the butt of jokes. You will most certainly embarrass your family at an English wedding if you do so."

Dan sighed. "Well, what's wrong with my belt? It's custom-made."

Her face became devoid of expression. "I strongly advise leaving that here. I'm sure the other guests will remember your name without having to read it over your backside."

He didn't particularly care for her dry tone. "It's a Western tradition. In fact, I'm having two belts made for Claire and her new husband as sorta 'stocking stuffer' wedding gifts."

"I beg your pardon?"

"One's gonna say 'bride' and the other'll say 'groom.' In script, which is real hard for the guy to do."

Lilia opened her mouth but no sound came out. He guessed that meant she didn't think the belts were a good idea.

"Of course, I'll get them something silver as the real gift. I was hoping you'd help me choose."

She nodded. "I'd be happy to do that. Anyhow, Shannon will help with wardrobe, as I mentioned, while you and I get down to work on polite conversation, correct table manners under all sorts of circumstances and ballroom dancing. You mentioned a steeplechase, I believe? I assume you know how to ride?"

"I was practically born in a saddle."

"Yes, but have you ridden English style before?"

"Hell, no. Little velvet caps and silly britches aren't my style. And I use a real man's saddle."

"Have you ever taken fences, Dan?"

"Taken 'em? I've *mended* fences."

A frown marred her smooth forehead. "You do realize that during a steeplechase you'll be expected to jump over obstacles? Very large obstacles?"

Dan scratched his head. "Yeah. I've never figured out that part. Seems dumb to me. Why not just go around 'em?"

"It takes a very good seat and firm hands and lots of practice…"

"I'm not too worried."

"Riding lessons, English saddle," Lilia said firmly, writing it down on a monogrammed notepad.

He curled his lip. "You're not gettin' me in those bun-hugger pansy pants or a velvet hat."

She waved a dismissive hand at him and continued to write. "We'll go see Jean Pierre for some dancing lessons, and then you and I can practice every day… Oh, and we'll need to schedule a manicure for you."

"Come again? Did you say 'manicure'?"

"Yes, Dan, I did. Your nails are ragged and your hands are in bad shape. I'm even going to suggest a paraffin wax treatment."

"Get outta here," he exclaimed.

"I beg your pardon?"

"You're yanking my chain, right? I'm not going to some salon for a—"

"Yes, you are. And we're also going to schedule you a haircut with Enrique right away. Plus I'll set you up with some light reading—etiquette books that you'll need to read and study every night over the next two weeks."

"I watch ESPN at night, and *COPS,* and the History channel. Bad movies. True crime shows."

"Not for the next fourteen days, Dan. Remember Cary Grant. Otherwise you'll be wasting your money."

He groaned.

She eyed him sympathetically. "You're very sweet to do this for your sister, you know. You must love her very much."

He looked down at the scarred hands that had proudly wielded shovels, hammers and rifles. Hands that had delivered calves and foals, mended fences and steered two-ton trucks. Beer-drinking hands. For Claire, they were shortly to be defiled by a manicure. Ugh.

"My sister was about the one bright spot in my life, growing up. And you know what's funny? I thought I'd hate her. But I fell in love with that little girl the minute I saw her."

"You thought you'd hate her? May I ask why?"

Dan sighed. "It's complicated."

She nodded and he stood up. "Well, it's been a long day, Miz Lilia. I think I'd like to go find my hotel room and take a hot shower. Enjoy my last night of television before being brainwashed by Emily Post."

Her lips twitched. "No such luck. I have reading material to give you right away." And his elegant little tormentor pulled a fat three-ring binder out of a filing drawer. She handed it to him with a wry smile. "Let the brainwashing begin."

Dan accepted it with a scowl and picked up his duffel. "It's been real nice meeting you. I can't wait to be transformed into a gentleman with a capital G. And I am sorry about destroying your china and your chair."

"That's all right. I'll survive." She smiled at him. "This won't be so bad, you know."

He scrubbed a hand over his bristly jaw and moved toward the door of her office. Then he turned and winked. "If I come in here tomorrow claiming whiplash, will it get me another kiss?"

She stared at him, an odd expression on her face. "No, Mr. Granger, it will not."

AFTER WALKING HIM out to the front door, Lil stared after the man, watched his jaunty, confident stride and the way he swung the duffel by a couple of fingers on the way out to his rental car. She shouldn't be ogling him, but she enjoyed the view of his broad shoulders and the quite magnificent male bottom under that dreadful belt.

His stance was cocky and casual. Nothing elegant or cosmopolitan about him. He had two inch-wide strips of hair growing shaggily down his neck in the back, evidence of how long it had been since he'd had a haircut.

He didn't have a clue how to conduct himself outside of a barn. And she loathed the instant presumption of familiarity that he'd assumed with her.

Yet she found his sheer unselfconsciousness sexy. He was more than comfortable in his own skin, unfettered by convention. A normal man, after wreaking havoc in his etiquette consultant's office and springing an erection (she even whispered that word *mentally*) should have run from there, mortified.

This man just took it all in stride and capped it all off by kissing her! He simply refused to accept the fact that he was a...buffoon. An extraordinarily handsome one, but a buffoon nevertheless.

He couldn't possibly be serious about the matching bride and groom belts, could he?

Granger tossed his carry-on into the passenger side of the rented red Mustang he was driving. His biceps bulged, straining against the short sleeves of his T-shirt. He got into the car himself.

Good Lord. She couldn't deny that she wanted to see him without his shirt again. She touched her lips, which were still sensitive after being scrubbed by that golden bristle of his.

From behind the windshield, he followed the gesture with his eyes and grinned, his white teeth flashing in the fading sunlight.

Lil dropped her hand as if burned, swung around on one of her kitten-heels and walked back to her office.

Shannon was on the phone and Jane appeared to be gone for the day, so Lil had a few moments to get herself together and think about how to proceed.

Why on earth had she allowed the man to kiss her? She hadn't kissed anyone since Li Wong, and he'd been out of her life for months now. Kissing Li had been unexciting. He had cold, squishy lips that were always too moist. She'd imagined, toward the end of things between them, that her damp kitchen sponge would provide more of a thrill.

She got more of a charge out of just looking at Dan's mouth than she'd gotten from touching Li anywhere. Li was smooth, hairless…flaccid. The man did have perfect manners—when one wasn't rejecting his munificent marriage proposals—and lovely suits, however. He even wrote thank-you notes.

Dan's bottom lip had a tiny indentation in the middle, a cleft just like the one in his chin. It was wildly sensual-looking, that split. His mouth looked uninhibited, casually wicked, and not squeamish about its destinations. Dan was a man who knew the secret of how to have fun.

Lil was starved for fun. *That's why I let him kiss me.*

She scolded herself for it. *You are a thirty-year-old business owner who specializes in decorum, Lilia! The age to have had fun was in high school, college—when everyone else your age was having it. This is neither the time nor the place to discover your inner hedonist…*

But in high school and college she'd been taking care of a frail, exceedingly proper grandmother in her seventies. Nana Lisbeth had raised Lil apart from her own generation; teaching her embroidery and watercoloring and French while most girls her age played school sports, went to rock concerts and snuck out to bars with fake ID's.

Nana had been Lil's entire world except for Jane and Shannon…but now Lisbeth London had been laid to rest beside Sir Henry. Even so, Lil went home to her empty house each night expecting to find her sipping lemon tea sweetened by a half-teaspoon of honey and letting a fresh crumpet go stale on a Royal Doulton plate.

She simply could not believe that she'd never see Nana Lisbeth again, never drop another kiss on her powdery cheek or smell rose-water mixed with the scent of old wool. How had a simple knee-replacement surgery led to a life-threatening infection?

With all that modern medicine could do, when it was someone's time, it was her time.

Shannon said goodbye to whomever she'd been talking to and Lil heard the click as she replaced the cordless phone in its cradle. Her modern rolling chair squeaked as she stood up. Seconds later she popped her head into Lil's office.

"So how did things go…" her voice trailed off as she saw the fragments of Lil's visitor's chair. "Oh. Not well, I see. My God, what else did he break?"

Lil brushed a bit of dark thread from the sleeve of her white suit jacket. "Just every conversational rule in the book, most of the boundaries of good taste and almost his neck."

Shannon laughed. "Got your hands full, huh?"

"You might say so."

"Juicy details?" Shan begged.

"If we can go for a drink and you'll take off that obnoxious, electric-blue jacket before I go blind."

"My goodness, Lil, but that was downright rude." Shannon chuckled and twisted her long, curly hair up into a knot on her head. She snagged a pen from Lil's desk to secure it.

Lil opened her drawer, pulled out a green plastic ballpoint and handed it to her friend. "Give the Waterman back, please."

"Oh, all right." Shan pulled the high-dollar pen out of her hair and shoved in the el cheapo. She dropped the expensive one back on Lilia's desk.

Lil picked it up, pulled two long curly blond hairs out of the pocket clip and grimaced. "You and Jane are rude to me all the time, anyway. So I have to return the favor. It's part of the beauty of our friendship." She dropped the hair into her wastebasket.

"Come on, I'll buy the cosmos," Shannon said, tossing her car keys in the air and catching them again.

"Is your car clean?" Lil asked. "Or does it still smell worse than the canals in Venice?"

"Hal had it detailed from top to bottom and it's daisy-fresh now."

"That man is a saint." Speaking of which, why were her thoughts turning back to the mouth of a sinner? Lil had a feeling she'd see that mouth swooping down on her all night, in her dreams.

5

THEY DROVE to Max a Mia, one of their favorite local places in nearby Avon, and Shannon ordered them two cosmos over Lil's protests.

"You know I can't drink those things. I'll lose my mind after one."

"So what? The mind should be lost every once in a while. It always finds its way home. Now drink up and tell me about the mad, naked Texan in your office."

Lil pulled the maraschino cherry out of her drink and bit into it. Full of red dye number-whatever and chockful of nasty chemicals, maraschino cherries were her weakness and the main reason why she didn't turn down the cosmo.

"I'll ask the waitress for a dish of them," Shannon said. "Remember that time at Jane's house? We were about ten. When you put so many of them on your sundae that it turned pink and looked bloody?"

Lil wrinkled her nose. "Yuck. Thanks for reminding me. But I loved them, and Nana wouldn't buy them. She called them 'radioactive abominations.'"

"Yeah. Nana had some really funny names for things."

"All the Bing cherries I could eat," sighed Lil, "but no delicious chemicals or preservatives."

"The cruelty," Shannon said. "Excuse me, Annie? Can we have a dish of cherries and another one of Spanish olives? Thanks, you're a doll."

Lil took a cool, burning sip of her drink and dropped another cherry into it when Annie came by with two little bowls. "I'm marinating it for later," she told Shannon.

"Yeah, whatever." Shan sucked the pimento out of one of the large olives.

"That's disgusting."

"I know. So tell me all about that golden moment when you were down on your knees in front of Cowboy, and he was shoving money at you?"

"You would bring that up. He had just broken one of Nana's cups and saucers. He wanted to buy a whole new set, since he knows how much 'us womenfolk' like matching sets of things."

"Ah. And he thought that a couple hundred bucks would spring for an antique, hand-painted set of Royal Doulton? He's a royal dolt."

"He's not that bad." Lil found herself defending the man. "And it was more like a couple thousand dollars he had in his hand. There were at least twenty one-hundred dollar bills. It was a fat wad."

"Tacky." Shannon popped another olive into her mouth and sucked on the entire thing.

"That's disgusting, too. And the sound effects are… salacious."

Shan just grinned. "You should see me with a stalk of celery, or a nice, long carrot."

"No, I shouldn't. You grew up in a nice home, with a mother who's a lady. Where did she go wrong?"

"You ever given a blow job, Lil?"

Her jaw dropped open. "That's none of your business! I can't believe you just asked me that."

"You haven't, have you."

"I—I—I'm leaving."

Shan put a hand on her arm. "I'm sorry. Don't go. I'll behave. I promise."

Lil exhaled a breath and reached for her drink, tipping more into her mouth than she meant to. She sputtered, partially choked and swallowed the liquid.

Shannon's wicked green eyes evaluated her to make sure she wasn't really in trouble. When she decided that Lil was okay, she lifted her glass in a toast. "To good manners."

Lil squinted at her, trying to decide what she was up to. She didn't really feel like drinking to good manners, all of a sudden. There was gentle mockery in her friend's tone—mockery that Lil was all too familiar with, and had been for years.

"I'm not Martha Stewart with a gun!" she declared.

"I never said you were, sweetie."

"I'm not the Princess of Purity." Lil picked up her glass and tossed the rest of the liquid back. Maybe it would douse her strange, unexplained lust for the cowpoke.

Shannon ordered another round. Then she said, "I've never called you that."

"Everyone else did at school. I don't mean to make anyone uncomfortable or on-edge around me," Lil said. "But they always are. Why? I may be an etiquette consultant, but I'm not a nun! And I don't mean to judge other people's behavior."

"I know that. You certainly don't repress me." Shan grinned. "Not that it's possible."

"And furthermore—" Lil took a big, angry gulp of her second cosmo "—I'm not as pure and uptight as you might think! Li and I once—" She felt her cheeks catch fire. "We once—well, you know. In the living room, with all the lights on."

Across the table, Shannon's mouth worked.

Lil wondered if she'd gotten a bad olive.

And then her friend put her elbows on the table, folded her arms and let her head drop onto them. Her shoulders began to shake.

"Are you…? Are you *laughing* at me?" Indignantly Lil gulped even more of her drink.

Shannon shook her curly head, gave an audible gasp and kept shaking.

"*Crying* for me?"

She shook her head again.

"Then what?"

Finally she raised her head. "Oh, Lil," she said unsteadily. "You've just been so protected from the world. Look, I know you don't like to share these kinds of things, and Jane and I never dared ask you, but is Li the only guy? That you've ever…?"

Lil compressed her lips. She wanted very badly to lie.

Very, very badly. *How do I explain to my former Great Slut childhood friend, who's been an actress out in L.A., that yes, I am a virtual virgin? That I was going to wait until marriage, and finally got so curious that I couldn't? That it didn't seem to matter so much because I was positive I'd marry Li?*

How do I explain that I've heard her talk about vibrators a million times, but never actually seen one? I'm pathetic. I belong in another century. But I'm stuck in this one.

Lil drained her second cosmo in a very unladylike couple of gulps. Then she nodded.

"That's what I thought. And it's a crime."

"A crime?"

"What if you had married that creep?" Shannon signaled for yet another round of drinks.

"Oh, no—I couldn't." Lil's head was swimmy already, and more alcohol was a very bad idea. Besides, a lady never, ever had more than two drinks in public.

"Have another cherry, sweetie. Or two."

"Okay." Lil looked at the cute, happy little cherries in the shallow dish. "Which one of you wants to be next? You, the little plump one, or you, with only half a stem? Aha. I feel sure that it's you, my little vixen! With the dent in your side…" She popped it into her mouth and looked up to find Shannon grinning. "What?"

"Nothing. My olives are getting pushy, too."

"You've got to keep them in line," Lil said solemnly.

"Very true. Oh, thank you, Annie!"

The waitress set two more long-stemmed glasses in front of each of them. "You celebrating something, girls?"

Lil smiled, fascinated by how Annie's chandelier earrings caught the light. "Pretty," she murmured.

"Yes, we're celebrating." Shannon nodded. She raised her glass. "To the end of the innocence!"

Lil lifted her own glass very slowly, focused on keeping the pink liquid within the rim. "To lend of inner sense," she exclaimed, pleased that she hadn't spilled any.

She laughed along with Shannon, wrapped in a warm, happy glow.

"LIKE THIS?" Lil asked, an hour later. She wobbled a little on Shannon's red velvet couch. Normally she thought the thing was beyond vulgar, since it was squishy and shaped like a pair of huge lips. Tonight it didn't seem bad.

"Yes, just like that. Now watch." Shannon looked like a beautiful, kinky Bugs Bunny wielding that carrot.

Lil collapsed into a fit of giggles and managed to shove the tip of her own carrot up one of her nostrils. "Ick!"

Shannon took it away from her and handed her another one. Then she put hers between her lips and took it into her mouth. She settled her lips around it into an O. Then she gripped it firmly in one fist and moved it in and out of her mouth, in and out. She raised her brows in an indication that Lil should do the same.

Lil inserted her own carrot.

"Push it back farther," commanded Shan.

"Gaahh."

"Now, tight with your lips."

"Ooooog."

"Pull. Push. Pull. Push."

It was an absolutely ludicrous sight. Lil disintegrated into giggles again. Her head fell between her knees and the carrot dropped onto the floor.

Shannon sighed. "How many bags are we going to go through? Jeez!"

"Your face…it's so shilly-looking! How can a man kleep a straight face?" Lil gasped for air.

"I can promise you, they're not focused on your face. They are slobbering with gratitude and their eyes are shut."

"Good thing!"

"Okay. I can tell that your motor skills are toast. But you get the general idea."

"Hee hee hee hee!"

"Yeah. Now, remember what I told you about the underside and the root. And the balls."

"Root-balls!" Lil chortled.

Shannon bit the end off her carrot and shook her head, crunching away.

"Wanna root-ball float?"

"Definitely not. But you go ahead and help yourself."

"Hookay…"

"You probably won't remember any of this in the morning, but maybe some of it will sink into your subconscious. I think maybe the cowpoke is a good candidate—but only if he's very generous himself. Got that?"

"Cowpoked! Hee hee hee."

"Exactly. You go get yourself cowpoked."

THE SUN was an evil squirt of vitriolic mustard in her eyes. Lil moaned and tried to blink it out, but it only spread. Her stomach felt as if someone had poured gasoline into it and set it on fire. And she wanted to be sick on top of that. Oh, Heaven help her. She rolled to her side and discovered that was a mistake, since it was a long way down to the floor from her four-poster bed and looking at the floor from this angle made her queasy. The patterns in the oriental rug down there spun into a kaleidoscope of nausea.

When she opened her eyes again, she saw that she'd slept in her suit skirt, stockings and blouse—disgusting.

How had she gotten home last night? Lil didn't remember. She'd gone out to Max a Mia with Shannon, she'd eaten a bowl full of maraschino cherries. She'd *spoken* to the cherries and Shan had laughed at her.

Then something about carrots?

Lil bolted upright. *Oh, no. No!*

Her memory was surely playing tricks on her. But there in her mind's eye was Diabolical Bugs, playing with her carrot.

Push. Pull. Push. Pull.

You've never given a blow job, have you, Lil?

"I'm going to kill her with my bare hands," she whispered. She slid, inch by painful inch, off her bed until she was standing upright. She clung to a bedpost for support. "I'm going to knock her out with a single blow to the head from Emily Post!"

Lil staggered into the bathroom and slumped to the floor near the toilet. *So this is what everyone meant by worshipping the porcelain god.*

"I'll never drink again," she moaned.

Yeah, all the girls at school had said that, too, looking green and shaky but secretly proud.

What in the name of Heaven was there to be proud of?

Lil laid her forehead against the cool lid and debated whether or not she had to relieve her bladder or her stomach first. She decided to let them argue about it while she went back to sleep sitting up.

She jerked awake at an image of Nana Lisbeth, blinking her pale blue eyes at her in shock. Nana put one hand to her temple and the other to her heart as Lil moved a carrot in and out of her mouth.

Oh, Lord. How much was truly seen by those who'd passed on? Did they look down as their relatives made wicked fools of themselves on earth? Horrid, horrid thought.

Lil struggled to her feet and reflected that even ghosts must practice some sort of etiquette. Surely it wasn't acceptable behavior for a ghost or an angel to peer into the privacy of someone's bedroom or bathroom? For goodness' sake!

She hung onto a towel bar and slowly peeled off her blouse, bra, skirt and stockings. She stumbled over to the shower and turned it on full-blast.

With shaking hands, she found some ibuprofen, took four of them, and noted with gloom that the circles under her eyes were much larger than her breasts.

She vaguely recalled Shannon telling her to go get herself cowpoked. Oh, very nice, Shan. And out of the question.

Blearily Lil climbed into the shower and let the water thunder down on her head in the hopes of achieving some clarity and sense. Instead it filled her ears and made her sneeze. It steamed her brain and only made it swell larger than its too-small cavity. Ugh.

Lil shut off the water once she'd achieved the basics of soap and shampoo. She stood on the tile feeling like death until she remembered that one's customary next step on ending a shower was to grab a towel.

She'd much rather crawl back into bed—who cared if she was naked and wet. But instead, she had to get dressed, perk up and prepare to deal with Granger and his wicked mouth.

Her breasts tingled at the thought. She told them to stop immediately. She went to her lingerie drawer and pulled out a beige bra and a new pair of stockings. She sat on Nana's vanity stool and pulled them on, wondering why the good-quality department store ones cost so much. Hadn't she heard something about the invention of a pair of panty hose that would never run? But big industry had firmly squashed the idea, since there was so much money to be made off of women....

Soon her nudity was hooked, strapped and control-topped. She pulled another suit out of her closet, this one beige, and put it on with a white camisole and beige-and-white spectator pumps with a low, elegant heel. She fastened Nana's pearl earrings at her lobes, swept her hair into a French twist and added just a touch of pink gloss to her mouth.

Because her skin color was pale green this morning, she swept her cheeks with a faint dusting of blusher and blotted the perspiration on her lip and forehead with loose powder.

Lil stopped on the way to work for two quarts of cold water. She should put something into her stomach to soak up the leftover alcohol, but nothing appealed to her.

She pulled into the parking lot of Finesse in her Camry and noted with something akin to despair that the red Mustang was already there. Wonderful.

She clicked in her kitten heels to the glass door between the elegant urns and juggled the cold water bottles and her purse as she reached for the handle. The door opened and slammed her in the kneecap.

Reeling from the pain, Lil clenched her teeth over the epithets that tried to get past them and vaguely registered Dan Granger's face, hidden behind a greasy paper fast-food wrapper.

"Haaaaaaaa," he said, around whatever was in his mouth. "Oh, dang, did I get your knee? And here I was trying to be polite, Lilia."

"Thank you," she managed. She hobbled into the reception area and was immediately assaulted with a disgusting smell. She braced herself on the reception desk, choking back bile. Ugh! Greasy Mexican food, and egg, and some awful combination of fried sweet peppers and onion.

Heaven help her, she was going to be—

Lil dropped her purse and water bottles and ran for the facilities.

6

DAN STOPPED MUNCHING and stared. "Was it something I said?" He bent to pick up the water bottles and the handbag and placed them on the reception desk.

Lilia's tall, blond partner emerged from the kitchen and sniffed the air before shooting him a cat-eyed smile. "So that's why it smells like taco hell in here."

She was gorgeous, loudly dressed in a screaming yellow leather jacket, and she appeared very amused.

Dan blinked twice at the jacket and fished his Oakley's out of the neck of his T-shirt. He settled them onto his nose and sighed with relief. "That's better."

She laughed.

"What's wrong with Miz Lilia?" he asked the Amazon.

"She's feeling a little under the weather. I took her out to a bar last night and she's not used to much alcohol."

"Ohhhhh." Light dawned on Dan. "You have the gal doing tequila shooters or something? She looks like *one* would put her under the table. Anyway, I have just the thing for her—a breakfast taco. It'll fix 'er right up. Eggs, cheese, fried potato, onion and hot sauce. Shocks the belly into submission and soaks up the booze."

"You don't say." The Amazon wrinkled her nose.

She was too perfect-looking for Dan. Professional beauty, he called it. Over the top. And he also didn't care for the way she swung her hips. This one was no Audrey. She carried herself as though she'd been around the block a few times. But she wasn't flirting with him, he'd give her that.

He preferred the challenge of Lil's...purity. She had that china doll quality that just stabbed him right in the groin. Made him feel like a dirty, bad boy for thinking about what she had on under that knee-length skirt. The forbidden turned him on. Feeling dirty turned him on. Exotic turned him on. Those dark eyes...

"I'm not sure that Lilia likes that kind of—" The blonde broke off as Lil returned to the room. "You okay, sweetie? I don't believe I've ever seen that particular shade of green on a human face."

"Shannon," his etiquette consultant said evenly, "you are evil. You should be listed as the eighth deadly sin— and *what* is that foul stuff you're drinking?"

Dan had wondered the same thing. It was reddish brown and mucky and unappetizing.

The Amazon swirled the nasty liquid in her glass. "Carrot juice."

Lilia choked and, to Dan's amazement, turned bright red. What was up with that? Who blushed at the mention of vegetable juice? Why?

"Mr. Granger," she said crisply. "Why don't we go to my office? Would you like a cup of coffee?"

"Only if I can have it in a cardboard cup, ma'am."

Her lips twitched as she turned to walk down the hallway, giving him another chance to admire that miracle of a derriere.

She swept into her office and up to her desk, saying, "A big strapping man like yourself can't be afraid of a little china." She stopped as she saw a tall plastic bottle of organic carrot juice on her blotter.

"Excuse me for a moment, won't you? I'll get your coffee and be back momentarily." Her words were polite, but he caught a glimpse of steel in the set of her chin.

"Surely."

She swiped the carrot juice and departed, giving him yet another opportunity to—

"Mr. Granger! Stop ogling that, please."

What, did the woman have an eye in her spine? But Dan just chuckled, saw that she'd placed a sturdy wing chair where the little matchstick one had been the day before, and sat in it. He finished his breakfast taco, set one on her desk as the polite thing to do and threw his wrapper and napkin away.

He noticed that his hat still adorned the head of the old coot on her credenza, and he got up and plucked it off. A second look at the old coot revealed that the bust was almost certainly of Sir Henry London. *Aw, hell.*

What had he said yesterday about how the *pompous ass* looked good in it? He closed his eyes for a moment. Then he turned and hung his hat off one of the wings of the chair before settling into it again.

Lilia glided into the room without the carrot juice or the martial light in her eye. She set another delicate flowered cup and saucer in front of him and he eyed it uneasily.

Then her nostrils flared and she turned even greener, if that were possible, when she saw the breakfast taco on her desk. "What's that?" she asked in a faint voice.

"Why, it's your breakfast taco, Lil. You scarf that down and you'll be right as rain, as my grandpa Lou used to say. It'll soak up all the acid, sit like a tasty brick in your tummy and keep you on-task."

"Breakfast *taco?*" She backed away from it as if the thing might spring at her and clamp onto her throat.

"Yeah. I was getting a couple for myself at this great little dive place, and I brought you one, too. Only polite, right? Oh, and here." He dug some little packets of hot sauce out of his jeans. "Regular and extra-spicy."

"That was…very thoughtful of you, Dan. But I'm feeling a bit queasy at the moment. A stomach virus, you know."

"Would that be another one of your little white lies? Blondie out there already told me you have God's own hangover, hon. So do what Uncle Dan says, now, and eat the cure."

"Shannon told you that I was—?" Her black eyes snapped.

"Aw, I woulda figured it out anyway. I'm experienced with that sort of thing." He grinned and leaned forward, unwrapping the taco for her.

She stared at it with naked revulsion. It stared back at her.

"Yummy," Dan said. "Here. Unroll the tortilla and add some sauce."

Miz London looked as if she'd rather eat roadkill, but

her manners got the better of her. He'd brought her a gift, and she would force herself to taste it.

Dan was impressed. She actually dredged up a polite smile, added the milder sauce and held the taco to her lips.

"Come on, it's not like it's something off of *Fear Factor*," he urged her.

She sank her small, pearly, ladylike teeth into the thing and took a bite. Her pretty pink lips wrapped around the corner of the soft taco. Dan knew he was staring, and remembered vaguely that it was rude, but he was mesmerized by the sight of her, in her French twist and pearls, with her mouth open wide around the phallic food.

She flushed as she looked up and caught him. He was quite sure his eyes were glazing over.

Her gaze flew from his and she chewed delicately, thoughtfully. "This is good," she said, sounding surprised.

"Of course it is. Would I lie to you?"

"If I can eat this taco in a greasy wrapper, then you can sip coffee out of that cup."

"But I'm afraid I'll break this one, too."

"And I'm afraid that I'll drop sausage, egg or grease onto my suit. We're both broadening our cultural horizons, here, Dan."

He grinned and picked up the cup and saucer. The china was so thin and delicate he could almost see through it. The cup rattled in the saucer as he tried to lift it by the tiny gilt handle, dwarfed between his rough thumb and forefinger. He held the rim to his lips and drank about a teaspoonful, since it surely couldn't be proper to gulp from a work of art like this.

The cup and saucer reminded him of Lilia; delicate, old-fashioned and lovely.

Meanwhile she tugged at the wax paper wrapper on the breakfast taco and tried to avoid spilling the contents even though the tortilla was inevitably springing holes.

If he looked half as ridiculous as she did, then they were quite the comedy show this morning.

Lilia ate about half of the taco before wrapping it back up. He was glad to see some color had returned to her face.

"Thank you, Dan." She dabbed at the corners of her mouth with a tissue that she'd put in her lap like a napkin. "That was very tasty."

He nodded and lifted the oversize thimble to his lips again in the hopes of putting an ounce more caffeine into his system. The tip of his index finger got stuck in the handle as he put it back into the saucer, and he had to shake it free. Meanwhile, the hot cup had burned his pinkie as he'd tried to support it. Damn the thing!

"Dan," she said. "Don't try to put your finger through the handle. Just hold it gently—you may use your third finger, too. And allow your fourth and fifth to spread outward like a fan. Your pinkie will extend in a little loop rather like the cup handle. None of your digits belong under the cup."

Digits? "I feel like a pansy," he complained.

"Just do it anyway." Lilia got up and went to a closet on the far side of the room. She took a folding card table out of it and refused his help in setting it up. Then she pulled a white, lacy tablecloth from a chest of drawers in the corner and unfolded it onto the table. Another drawer yielded a bunch of dishes and silverware, which she placed precisely in two place settings.

The crazy woman put three forks to the left of a large plate, two knives to the right of it, plus a big spoon and a weird little fork inside of it. Then at the top of the plate she added another spoon and another fork! Worse, she put a second little plate to the left of the big plate, and then four crystal glasses of varying shapes and sizes to the right of it. Dan blinked at the array. What in the hell did anyone do with all that, and more importantly, why?

She beckoned him over and reluctantly he came face-to-face with it all.

"All right, Dan. Now do you want to take a guess—"

"No. Just tell me. The only thing I know is that you eat off of the plate."

Lil smiled at him. "Actually the only thing on this table that you won't be eating from is the plate."

"Huh?"

"That large plate is known as a service plate. You'll use everything but the service plate, which will either be removed as the first course is served, or the first course will be served on a dish which goes on top of it."

"So it's useless? They just put it there to screw you up? Make you look stupid?"

She laughed. "Nobody's trying to make anyone look stupid. It's actually very simple. The general rule is to use each utensil, going from the outside of the plate toward the inside, as the courses are served."

"What about the fork and spoon at the top?"

"Those are provided for dessert, and yet another spoon would be brought for coffee after dinner. Sometimes you won't see the utensils at the top of the plate—it's a little more continental in nature than the typical American place setting. If you don't see them, then they'll be provided for you as dessert is served."

"What's the little munchkin fork for? The one inside the big spoon?"

"In this case, your first course is likely to be oysters. That's what the small fork is for. The next course will be soup, and you'll use the large spoon for that."

"I eat oysters from the shell."

"Not at a formal dinner, you don't. Slurping tends to be frowned upon—unless you're in China, but that's a whole other topic."

Dan frowned and shook his head. "And all the other forks to the left?"

"Salad—see the one thicker tine at the left? That's used for cutting large lettuce leaves if necessary. Try not to use a knife on salad."

"Why?"

"Just try not to. Now, the next fork is for fish, which is what the middle knife is used for as well. The inner fork and knife are for meat—the main course…"

Dan's eyes began to glaze over—this time from boredom and irritation, not from lust.

The glasses turned out to be for all different kinds of wine, and then one for water. Then there were napkin lessons. You put the darn thing in your lap a certain way. You dabbed with it, and never wiped the table with it.

You didn't spit anything into it, according to Lilia (though there were two schools of thought on how to remove a piece of fat or gristle from "one's" mouth, and some said hocking it into your napkin was okay).

Lilia advocated the palm to plate method, where "one" shoved the "offending morsel" under a "convenient bit" of parsley.

There were even frigging rules to follow when you were *done* with your damned napkin! He wasn't supposed to leave a napkin folded, since the implication then was that you thought your hosts might put it away without washing it. But he wasn't supposed to twist it or crumple it, either, because that would be untidy. He couldn't leave it on his chair—because that might indicate he was trying to steal the table linens.

"Oh, bullshit!" Dan exclaimed.

"I beg your pardon?" Lilia asked.

"This is ridiculous."

"You will refrain from cursing at the table, please. And from doing so in the presence of a lady."

"But—"

"Now, what do you do if you drop your napkin or it falls off of your lap?"

"Duh. Pick it up."

"No."

"Why the hell not?"

"You will leave it on the floor and signal the wait-staff that you need a fresh one—if they don't notice this on their own and take care of the problem right away. You'll signal them with eyes only."

"In other words, I don't yell 'Yo, dude!' in the middle of the conversation?"

"Exactly."

"So what *can* I do with my napkin at the end of the meal?"

"You will place it loosely to the left of your plate."

"Jeez. All these rules for a blasted square of cloth."

They talked about elbows, serving and removing, not blowing on anything to cool it off. She showed him what a finger bowl was, and how to use it. They discussed the proper way to pass salt—always with the pepper. And so on and so forth.

Dan began to yawn uncontrollably, having not slept well the night before. Lilia made him cover his mouth with his hand, to his annoyance.

"But if a yawn is the body trying to get more oxygen, then why would you block it?" he argued.

Finally she looked at her watch. "We have fifteen minutes to get you to your manicure appointment, Dan. Then we have an appointment for your suit and tuxedo. Finally we'll have dinner and practice all of this."

"Hooray," he muttered. He looked down to see if his balls were still attached. As far as he knew, they were still hanging tough, but after a manicure…well, he just didn't know.

"IS THIS REALLY necessary?" Dan asked as Lil dragged him into a pink and yellow Victorian with too much gingerbread trim.

She glanced at his hands. "Yes."

"I'm a guy. We don't do manicures."

"Lots of men get manicures."

"Not real men."

Lilia shook her head at him and stepped up to the reception counter. "Hi, Katy. We have an appointment for Dan Granger. He needs a paraffin dip, too. We need to try to get his hands into shape for a formal event in a couple of weeks."

"Okay. I'll let Tisha know you're here."

Tisha was a young lady of about nineteen who looked thrilled to be giving him any kind of treatment at all. She stuck his hands in two twin bowls of glass marbles and soapy water before digging at his cuticles and nail beds with various strange instruments and then filing and buffing his nails.

He was the only man in the place except for an old geezer getting a pedicure. The geezer looked blissful as a sweet young thing rubbed his gnarled old feet with lotion and tried not to gag at his funky, yellowed toenails.

Tisha sawed on some callouses of Dan's with a pumice stone and then had him walk over to a heated vat of apricot-colored liquid. She dunked each of his hands into it, once, twice, and then three times. It was hot wax, and he had to admit that it felt good.

Then she covered his hands with plastic baggies and shoved them into strange plastic pockets heated by electrical cords. She sat him down to wait for a few minutes while the wax "conditioned" his skin.

"Just call me Dansy the Pansy," he muttered to Lilia, clapping his white plastic paws together. She laughed.

Why am I doing this again? Oh, yeah. For Claire. Don't want to embarrass Claire in front of her Aristo-Cat. Damn him. And damn Louella, too, for putting him in this ridiculous position.

Lilia would tell him that it wasn't polite to damn his own mother. He supposed it wasn't. But why couldn't Louella just accept him the way he was?

Tisha stuck him back in front of her manicure desk and used the plastic bags to peel off all the apricot wax. Now his hands felt greasy. Wonderful.

She grabbed one and squirted lotion into the middle of it. Then she began a hand massage.

*Okay. This ain't bad at all…*he thought he might start to purr as the girl rubbed every muscle in his palm and then started working his fingers. In fact, this was really almost erotic. He closed his eyes and imagined it was Lilia doing the rubbing.

Ten minutes later she and Tish nudged him, interrupting a very interesting dream starring Lilia in a silver satin garter ensemble.

"Come on, Dan," she said. "Let's go and get you fitted for—what did you call it?—a penguin suit."

7

LILIA WONDERED if it was such a great idea to be taking Dan Granger to Nana Lisbeth's house for formal dinner training. It hadn't escaped her notice that he'd spent a good part of the day ogling parts of her that he had no business ogling, and the guy had even kissed her yesterday.

She didn't think he'd do anything she really objected to, but the more she was around him, the more his animal magnetism was getting to her. What if he did something that she *should* object to and she *didn't* object?

That was the problem. Lil didn't believe in even kissing a man until the third date, and yet she had already kissed Dan Granger—on the first day they'd met!—and pictured him naked several times. She'd had salacious thoughts about him. She'd even had a full-blown erotic fantasy while pretending to read a glossy women's magazine in the nail salon!

What in Heaven was wrong with her? The blame rested squarely with him: those biceps. Those triceps. Those pecs. The powerful chest. And that bulge that she kept sneaking peeks at, shameless hussy that she… wasn't.

She wished she could be more shameless. Modern

women just did what they wanted. This was the age of *Sex and the City*. Why couldn't she just be a modern woman? Channel an inner Samantha? Look at Shannon.

She should take a page out of Shannon's book. In so many ways, Lil was tired of Emily Post's book. Emily didn't have much fun, and Lil was pretty sure she'd never had anything as scintillating as an orgasm.

She'd been too busy making sure everyone followed a lot of rules that became even more obsolete with each passing minute.

She glanced at Dan out of the corner of her eye and tried not to giggle at the thought of the august Emily in the throes of a five-alarm orgasm.

Shannon had made an executive decision to take his suitcases, and everything inside them, to the Salvation Army without asking him. He was a little bit steamed, even though she'd replaced a lot of things already.

"I can't believe she did that!" he said again, as he took another right and then an immediate left onto Lil's street.

"I do apologize," Lil repeated. "She can get a little overbearing." She didn't say that it was all for the best, because most of his wardrobe dated from the early eighties and hadn't been of good quality to begin with.

"That's a hell of an understatement!" Dan growled. "Who does she think she is?"

"If it's any consolation, you're not the only one. Her boyfriend still hasn't forgiven her for throwing his clothes into a Dumpster. He almost threw her after them."

Dan pulled up to Nana Lisbeth's house as per Lil's

instructions, and she waited for him to come around the Mustang and open her door for her, as she'd taught him.

She swung her feet out, knees together, and took his extended hand to get out of the seat. It was so big and warm. She imagined it on her—

"Thank you." She tried to tug her fingers away from his, but just as he had the first time they'd met, he hung on. Judging from the electricity pulsing from his skin to hers, Dan Granger was the one man on the planet capable of giving Emily Post herself an orgasm. Well, if Miss Post had still been around.

Lilia almost slapped herself for allowing this kind of nonsense to run through her mind, but Granger's hazel eyes were vaporizing any intelligent thought before it had a chance to form. She wanted to lick him, and Lil had never licked anyone in her life—definitely not Li Wong.

She was quite sure that licking people was not good manners in any country.

"I have to get my keys," she said, and pulled her hand back. *You don't like cowboys. The Wild West bores you stiff even in the movies. You've been a Cary Grant and Sean Connery fan since you were ten. You like your men supersonically civilized. Why do you have the hots for a man who shovels manure?*

She didn't know. She couldn't explain it.

She found her keys and walked up the steps to Nana Lisbeth's—no, *her* front door, with the full knowledge that Dan Granger's eyes were fixated on her backside. Heat bloomed over her skin. And keeping Shannon and Samantha from *Sex and the City* in mind, she dropped her keys and then bent to pick them up, knowing that her skirt would pull tight as she did so.

She inserted the key into the lock and watched Dan, reflected in the glass of the door. He actually made a fist and stuck it in his mouth. She was pretty sure that was the man-sign for "hubba hubba" or something like that.

Smiling to herself, she entered the house and beckoned him in. She'd certainly never inspired Li Wong to stick his fist in his mouth, not that he would ever have considered doing such a thing. Lil almost snorted. It was time she admitted it: Li had been absolutely awful in bed.

Dan looked around at all of Nana's antiques, the crisp lace curtains and the little Victorian doilies scattered about. He seemed afraid to walk on the oriental rugs in his boots, and he looked rather oversized in Nana's house, like a human who'd stumbled into a hobbit's abode.

Dan actually winced when he came face-to-face with an oil portrait of Grandfather Henry.

"I, uh, didn't mean to call your grandpa a pompous ass," he said.

"I beg your pardon?"

"When you put my cowboy hat on him."

"Oh." She dimpled. "That's all right. I think he would have laughed. He had a good sense of humor."

Dan looked relieved.

"Would you like a glass of wine while I'm heating things up? I know you'd probably rather have beer, but part of tonight's lesson is learning about wine."

"Sure."

"I'm not a connoisseur, and neither will you be after only tonight, but we'll sample a chardonnay, a Pinot grigio, a cabernet and a French Bordeaux. Then we'll have a little port after dinner. Traditionally, at the end of a formal dinner, the women leave the table and the men linger over port or brandy and cigars. You may very well be doing that at your sister's wedding, and I want you to be comfortable."

She gave him a glass of wine and showed him how to hold it. She poured one for herself—thank God she was feeling human again and wouldn't have to go anywhere near vodka tonight—and then busied herself with heating the meal.

They'd picked it up from one of her favorite caterers, since she'd had no time to cook, and the table had been set since yesterday.

As she puttered, she invited Dan to take a seat or have a look around—whichever he felt more comfortable doing. He stuck his head into the dining room and visibly blanched at the elaborate table setting.

"It's not any worse than what you saw earlier," she told him. "I promise." She put on some classical music and he grimaced. "You'd better get used to that, too, Dan, because your ballroom dancing lessons begin tomorrow."

He sighed and tipped back his wine.

They began the first course, which was escargot, and once he'd gotten over his initial reaction to eating snails, he admitted that they were delicious.

Next she served him a different wine and a delicate watercress soup, teaching him how to sip it from the side of his spoon, never inserting the entire bowl of it into his mouth.

Following that was a crisp salad of field greens, walnuts and goat cheese. Dan declared he'd rather eat tufts of grass than that peppery-tasting hairy stuff called endive.

Lilia grilled him on what he should do if someone erroneously used his bread plate.

"Tell 'em what a moron they are?"

"No. Either don't eat any bread, or use the side of your dinner plate for it instead. Remember, manners exist to make others feel *comfortable,* not uncomfortable."

"And if they swipe my coffee cup, too?"

"Same basic principle. Don't embarrass anyone."

For the main course, she served crown roast of lamb with the French Bordeaux. She could tell that Dan itched to pick up the lamb morsels and gnaw on the bones, and truth to tell, she sympathized with him. But in the name of civilization, they used knives, forks and small, polite bites.

"This is delicious," he told her. "Better than any English food I've had, I'll tell you that much."

"It's from a French caterer. I avoid English food whenever possible," said Lil.

"Good girl. There are only so many ways to screw up a meal, but the Brits have mastered all of 'em."

She laughed. "But of course you won't share that opinion at an English dinner table."

"I won't? Okay."

"I don't mean to pry, Dan, but how did your mother and sister come to live in England?"

His expression grew sardonic. "Well, a man named Nigel Leighton happened to visit Amarillo on business about twenty-two years ago. He fell in love with my *very married* mother's face, and she fell in love with his accent, his worldly airs, his money and the promise of world travel. She ran off with him and left her husband and fourteen-year-old son behind."

"I'm so sorry."

"It's real funny how she's also left her accent and her working class roots behind, too. She's a true English primrose, now. But I happen to know how bad she misses biscuits n' gravy and tamales."

Lil sipped her Bordeaux and reflected ruefully that she liked California merlot much better, no matter how much she tried to train her palate.

Dan took a sip of his, too, and wrinkled his nose. "I'm sorry, but this stuff tastes like bitter dirt."

"It's very expensive, exclusive wine," Lil said, smiling. "But I agree with you."

"You do?"

"Yes. The French think that we Americans simply have unsophisticated palates, and it's probably true, but I've never acquired a true fondness for French Bordeaux. A good thing, since it saves me a lot of money." She got up to remove the dinner plates.

"I like you, Lilia." Dan said it suddenly. The candlelight turned the stubble on his face to gold, and lent metallic highlights to his wavy chestnut hair. "I like you a lot, and I expected not to. I thought you'd be some pretentious priss-pot. But you've got a nice, refreshing honesty under the whole Audrey Hepburn thing."

Audrey Hepburn thing? "Well, thank you, Dan." She took the plates and retreated into the kitchen with them. *I thought you'd be some pretentious priss-pot,* he'd said. *No—I'm an unpretentious priss-pot. How do you like that?*

She set the plates in the sink and ran water over them. *And I'm tired of being a priss-pot.* She picked up the glass of Chardonnay that she'd left virtually untouched and drained it.

What's the most proper, mannerly way to seduce someone? Where's Judith Martin's guide to excruciatingly correct bedroom behavior?

Lilia took out the key lime cheesecake she'd made two nights ago and garnished with such care. She prepared and started the espresso machine. Then she went back out to the dining room and joined the subject of her most unladylike lust.

How on earth did you get a man from the dining room to the bedroom with any kind of subtlety? She couldn't just grab him by the shirt collar and say, "You. Come with me."

She couldn't just whip off her blouse and spray herself with whipped cream, declaring, "I'm your dessert, you big stud." Shannon might, but there was no way that Lil could.

She supposed that she could just walk over and start kissing him on that sinfully cleft lower lip of his, but that didn't seem very subtle, either.

"What are you thinking about, Miz Lilia?" Dan looked at her lazily in the candlelight, swirling his wine.

Oh, wouldn't you like to know.

I'd like to lose my virginity all over again, but this time to a real man. A guy who knows what to do with it, and doesn't consider me some lowly half-breed only fit to scrub his floors!

Li's racism still boggled her mind. She'd encountered it before, but from Americans. She'd thought she'd be safe from that with Li. How wrong she'd been.

"What am I thinking about?" she repeated. "Just that I like you, too, Dan—hat, boots and all." She smiled. "Would you like coffee?"

"Yes, please. Just black."

She brought in the coffee and the key-lime cheesecake. "The only part of the meal that I actually made," she said, cutting him a thick slice.

He took a bite and his eyes widened. "Did I say I liked you? Because now I love you. This is incredible."

She flushed with pleasure. "It's my grandmother's recipe. This was her house."

"Did you lose her recently?"

Lil nodded and focused on her own slice of cheesecake. "Yes. A few months ago. She had a simple knee replacement surgery and though it was painful, she seemed to be doing well. But somehow the knee got infected and the infection got out of control—it was too much for her system. She was in her late eighties."

"I'm sorry for your loss."

"Thank you." She kept her response simple, not

wanting to reveal that losing Nana Lisbeth had in effect been losing her entire family in one day. That she still couldn't get used to living in this house without her, but couldn't bear to sell it, either. She felt as if she were the custodian for Nana's ghost.

He gestured around him. "I did wonder a little about the antiques and knickknacks. And the place even smells of another century." He clapped a hand over his mouth at her expression. "I didn't mean it smells bad—just kind of like an old person lives here."

"I know what you mean." Lilia forgave him. The musty scents were in the eighteenth-century upholstery, the nineteenth-century rugs and the well-worn pages of countless books. No matter how often she cleaned and lemon-oiled the furniture, the rooms of the house did retain those odors.

He took another hefty bite of his cheesecake and savored it, his eyes running lazily over her. "This place suits you in certain ways…"

"Are you calling me an antique?" she asked, with a smile.

"No! God, no. I just meant that you're a little old-fashioned."

"Uptight?"

"I didn't say that, now did I? Why, do you think you're uptight?"

She left her cheesecake untouched and focused on her coffee. "I—I don't want to be. But other people seem to think I am. I think it's how I was raised."

"Well, are you lookin' for someone to lower you,

now?" He cocked his head at her and grinned, clearly joking.

Lil took a deep breath and made up her mind. "Yes, Dan, I am."

He stared at her, his eyebrows raised in surprise. "Come again?"

She clenched her hands around her coffee cup and looked steadily into his eyes, which were now the color of good brandy. "I'm…tired of living like an old lady."

Dan laid his fork across his plate, prongs pointed at eleven o'clock, and touched his napkin to his mouth. "Lilia. I'm not real big on subtlety, and I don't want to get slapped, so I'm just gonna ask this straight out. Was that the invitation that I think it was?"

Still gripping the cup and unable to recall either the words or the intent behind them, she nodded.

He dropped his napkin to the left of his plate and leaned back in his chair, a wicked smile playing around those cowboy lips of his. "Well, then, darlin', I'd like to RSVP."

8

LIL SAT FROZEN in her chair as Dan stood to his full height of six foot two or so and came around the table. The truth was, she had no idea how to behave in these particular circumstances.

Dan didn't seem to find the situation awkward at all. He took two steps toward her, caught her hand and pulled her up. "You're not used to issuing invitations like that, are you, Lil?"

She shook her head and stared intently at the logo on his T-shirt, her heart pounding.

He tipped her chin up. "So why me? What does Miss Manners want with a rude rancher who don't know his butt from his elbow at a formal dinner?"

"I don't know."

"I don't know, either, but I think you're beautiful." And Dan put his big, warm, newly soft hands on either side of her face and kissed her.

He tasted of tart wine and lime, sweet cake and rich, dark coffee. He smelled of warm skin, an outdoorsy aftershave and male musk civilized by soap and laundry detergent. His lips parted hers and he delved into her mouth with a sure, skilled tongue that knew exactly what it was doing.

Li Wong had poked uncertainly at her tongue with his own, both of them vaguely wondering why. Li Wong had no part of this kiss, though, and she banished him as unworthy of comparison.

Dan rubbed his lips against hers in a sweet, sensual dance. He caught her bottom lip between his teeth and sucked at it before releasing it to wander to the corner of her mouth, where he licked gently and brushed his jaw against her cheek.

His mouth whispered up to her temple, down to her cheekbone, over to her ear. Her scalp tingled as he brushed a loose strand of her hair behind it, and she shivered at his breath, which awakened every tiny nerve ending north of her lobe.

Heat bloomed on her skin and spread throughout her body, even though the man hadn't touched her below the neck. His fingers threaded through her hair, obliterating the French twist so that it fell free around her shoulders.

"That's better," he murmured. "Gorgeous. So soft."

Like a cat, she curled her head into first one hand, then the other, helplessly craving more of his touch.

Then his lips were on hers again, awakening some response deep inside her that she hadn't even known existed. It flickered out of her and then spread throughout her body.

Her nipples tautened and hardened, begging for his hands and mouth. A very unladylike dampness spread between her thighs and a hot spot throbbed there, a strange sexual pulse.

It made her want things; dirty things that she wasn't accustomed to wanting. None of what she desired had any relation to etiquette.

Dan groaned and pulled her against him, moving his hands out of her hair, across her shoulders, down her spine. She felt that bulge of his, unmistakably hard, against her belly, and as he cupped her bottom she slid her own hands down to explore.

She heard his swift intake of breath as she brushed her knuckles down the thick, long ridge in his jeans and then wrapped her fingers around it.

His hands tightened on her rear, and his heat burned through the thin skirt and stockings—not the sexiest items, nor the easiest to get off. Lil bit her lip. If she'd known, she'd have put on the garter belt and thigh highs that she'd gotten last year in the hopes of spicing up Li's reaction to her. Instead he'd scoffed and told her she looked like a whore.

Now he'd say she was behaving like one, but she didn't care. It felt a lot better than the dismal prospect of becoming a repressed Chinese matron.

Dan enjoyed exploring her back there, and when he'd had enough he stroked up to her waist and then, yes! To her breasts. She let her head fall back as he cupped them, and he kissed her throat as his hands delved under her camisole and came into contact with her bare skin.

Deftly he unhooked her bra and slid up the camisole. He groaned at the sight of her breasts, bent his head and captured one in his mouth. Lil cried out at the contact, at the hot, wet suction of his lips, at the sensations that rushed from her nipple to the juncture of her thighs.

He stripped off the camisole and bra, then his own T-shirt, giving her another glimpse at his broad, bare chest and the muscles honed from long hours working outdoors. She went weak in the knees.

Dan bent toward her breasts again, took the other one into his mouth and backed her to the other end of Nana's heavy, mahogany dining room table. Before she realized what he was doing, he lifted her up and sat her on it, nestling himself between her legs and rucking up her skirt.

He kissed away her protest and went back to her breasts, palming them, rubbing them, plucking her nipples while she grew increasingly restless with need.

"I know, I know, darlin'," he said. "I'll give you what you want." Dan pushed her down onto the table, still standing between her legs, and ran his hands up her thighs until he was under her skirt.

The stockings were sheer and he could see straight through them, but they created a difficult barrier for him. He stroked all the way up to her mons, where she was helplessly damp, and played her there with the pad of his thumb.

She quivered and whimpered as he teased her, shifting her hips and biting her lip.

Finally, when she thought she would die, he slid his fingers under the very unsexy waistband of the hosiery. She expected him to pull them down, expected an awkward moment.

Instead he bent to kiss her lips again. Staring straight into her eyes, he ripped the stockings down the middle, dropped to his knees and settled his mouth right at the core of her.

He licked once, and she screamed, hoarse and helpless. He licked twice, and she rode a moan. He licked a third time, and she came apart. A tide of pleasure rushed over her and color burst behind her eyelids.

She fell to earth again and opened her eyes to find him watching her, still in position, and very pleased. The shreds of her stockings clung to her legs, which were draped over his shoulders, and candlelight flickered behind her. She started to get shocked at herself, spread-eagled on Nana Lisbeth's dining room table, doing dirty things with a complete stranger.

Then he put his mouth back on her and she bucked while he rumbled with amusement. She clutched at the sides of the table while his lips and tongue gave her impossible pleasure and she began to shake all over.

He pushed her thighs even wider and plunged deeper. He increased his range, moving from top to bottom of her cleft and then back to center, where he suckled until she exploded again and again and again.

Though she would have sworn she'd died, she came back to reality and lay spent while he chuckled.

"What…" she asked weakly. "What…?"

"That's called a multiple orgasm, darlin'." He got to his feet and put his hands on either side of her, grinning down. "Did you like that?"

She could only blink at him, dazed. Finally she nodded. "But—what about you?"

He laughed. "Well, I have to admit that Wally, here, is real, *real,* ready to come out and play with the beav." Dan unbuttoned his fly and slid his jeans off while Lil pulled off the embarrassing remnants of her stockings, taking a sneak peek. He was beautiful and huge. She'd never seen anything like it. And he was coming at her.

"I, um. Dan? I don't know if that—if it, is, um, going to—"

"It's okay. We'll make it fit. I'm not going to hurt you, I promise." He pulled her by the knees to the edge of the table again and took her hands. He put them on his cock and slid them up and down. It was velvety-soft at the tip, but muscular everywhere else. He showed her how to help roll on a condom while she simply marveled over his size.

Dan touched her between the legs with it, rubbed his moisture into hers, parted her. Her smallness was only a hindrance at first. He worked his way in very slowly, pleasuring her there with his hands and then cupping her bottom, tilting her back.

Amazingly enough, her body stretched to accommodate him and the fullness was blissful. When he was finally sheathed in her, he kissed her deeply, pushed her back onto the table again, and slid out a few inches. Then he pushed in again, into the warm fist that her body created for him.

As they established a rhythm, meeting thrust for thrust, she felt a different kind of tension building in her, and thrilled to it.

She clutched for the edges of the table again, feeling the cool, polished surface smooth under her bottom. Dan's hands found hers, though, and held them tightly as they both climbed together.

"I'm not gonna last, Lil, I'm sorry," he told her. "You feel so good…I'm only human…oh, yes!"

His rhythm quickened and intensified, his eyes shut, and he assumed an expression of half pleasure, half pain. Finally he pulsed within her, once, twice, three and four times, groaned helplessly and let his forehead fall to the table next to her neck.

Lil lay impaled and still dazed, pinned by his big body, quivering with yet another pent-up, not yet released climax. *It's okay,* she thought. *Because I'm not sure I can stand another one. I think it might really kill me.*

"I'm sorry," he said into her ear. "I couldn't hold on anymore."

She started to say that it was all right…but he moved out an inch or so and she tensed and quivered. He glanced at her face, pushed the hair away from her forehead. Then, touching his tongue to hers and sucking her bottom lip into his mouth he slid back in and ground the root of himself against her in an excruciatingly slow circle.

He pulled her hard against him, his fingers once again under her bottom, and rocked. The inner contact and the outer contact at once worked a magic of some kind, and she convulsed around him in yet another shower of pleasure, unintelligible sounds coming from her own throat.

"Atta girl," said Dan. "Now I don't feel quite so guilty."

Lil couldn't even hold her own legs around him any longer. She would have let them fall, but he hooked his elbows under her knees so that they couldn't. She lay satiated, like a blob of jelly, gazing up at Nana Lisbeth's crystal chandelier. She supposed she should be embarrassed, but she honestly couldn't muster the energy.

"You're so beautiful," he told her, looking first at her face and then between her thighs. "Down there, too. All pink and plump and pretty."

She flushed and tried to close her knees. Exactly what could he possibly think was attractive about that area?

She'd marveled over the sheer ugliness of it as a teenager, wondering what drew men to it at all. She'd finally decided it must be just the feel of it, because nobody could possibly want to get near the thing.

Yet Dan had…she shut her eyes. And she'd let him! He wasn't letting her close her knees, now, either.

"You embarrassed?" he asked.

Duh. She licked her lips. "Yes."

"Why? It's part of nature."

I'm not too sure about that. I've never heard of cows or horses having oral sex… But she didn't say it aloud.

"God wouldn't a put it there if we weren't supposed to enjoy it, Lil. I sure enjoyed it. How 'bout you?" He grinned down at her and finally pulled out, taking her hand and helping her to sit up.

She wasn't sure her joints would work again, and as she slid off the table her legs were still trembling. She tucked her hair behind her ears, not sure what to say other than an inane, "Wow."

Finally she looked at him shyly and said, "Well, Dan, I can't teach you to be any more of a gentleman in the bedroom, can I?"

He laughed and looked down, suddenly modest. "I have always had a policy of 'ladies first'—even if we're in the dining room."

She cringed as she saw Sir Henry's portrait, which hung next to the curved china cabinet, bulging with Royal Doulton and Meissen. Was it her imagination or was his white hair standing up more than usual? "I can't believe…"

"What?" He followed her gaze. His mouth twitched. "How's it hangin', bud?" And Dan saluted Sir Henry.

"We…in front of him, and on my grandmother's dining room table!" Lil put her hands to hot cheeks and found her camisole and skirt.

"You don't think she'd approve?"

Lil choked.

"Maybe you should hire me to *un*civilize you, then. Because there are all kinds of places far more shocking than that, babe. You ever done it in a public place?"

Her eyes flew to his, startled. "No!"

"Would you like to?"

"No! I couldn't possibly—"

"Sure you could." He grinned at her like the devil himself. "You can do it in a car. You can do it in a bar. You can do it anytime, or even with a twist of lime."

Lil began to laugh. "I didn't know you were a poet."

"Robert Frost, eat your heart out." He waggled his eyebrows evilly. "You can have sex on a plane, you can have sex on a train. You can have it in the breeze, you can have it wearing skis!"

She groaned, then thought about it. "Actually I don't think that's possible, Dan…"

He ignored her. "You can have sex at a fair, you can have sex anywhere! You can do it with a clown, or even while you wear a crown…"

"Enough. Here, put on your pants."

"Sex will put a smile on you, so you should go and have some, too!"

"Are you done, yet?"

He mock-frowned at her. "I'm starting to get the feeling that you don't appreciate my way with words."

Lil stepped into her skirt and zipped it up. She pursed her lips. "I appreciate your way with women a lot more."

He yawned and stretched his hands over his head to crack his back.

Her mouth went dry at the sight of all that lovely muscle in motion, held taut for her viewing pleasure. Then she noticed how incongruous this naked cowboy looked standing in front of her grandmother's sideboard, showcasing his penis next to Nana's cut crystal punch bowl.

"Pants!" she said. "You've got to put your pants on." Dear God, what if Nana had been looking down from above? The woman whose graciousness and reputation she'd always tried to live up to…

"Why are you in such a hurry, Miz Lil? The night is young. I have about as much use for my jeans right now as I have for that skirt you're wearing. Did I say you could put that back on? I don't believe I did."

She arched a brow and stuck her head through her camisole. "I didn't realize that I had to ask your permission."

"Here in Uncivilization 101, you gotta do as the alpha dog says."

She forgot her manners even further and stuck her tongue out at him—as though he were a good friend like Shannon or Jane.

"Rule number two of Uncivilization 101. You are not allowed to stick your tongue out unless you plan to use it on the alpha dog's bod."

"And what's rule number three?"

"Rule number three is that once you invite the barbarian to ravage you—"

"Ravish," she corrected.

"—you can't put on your skirt again until he says so, though he does appreciate the fact that right now you have it on with no panties." Dan took two long strides toward her and grasped the hem, pulling it upward and kissing her.

She could smell herself on him, and it should have horrified her but it didn't. She fell into the kiss for a moment, but then remembered—she couldn't do this again in front of these photographs and knickknacks. It made her too uncomfortable.

She engaged in a little tug-of-war with him over her skirt; pulling it down as he tried to raise it. "My bedroom," she whispered. "I can't—" She broke away from him and made for the stairs.

He caught up with her at the foot of them. "Rule number four of Uncivilization 101. Bedrooms are ho-hum. Do it anywhere but in a bed." His arm snaked around her and pulled her back against his chest. With the same hand, he cupped her breast almost roughly and rubbed her nipple with his thumb.

His other hand went directly under her skirt, searing her flesh everywhere he touched, moving from her bare buttocks to her inner thighs and then upward into the very light sprinkling of hair at her core.

Lil sagged against him, and then found herself grasping the newel post as he bent her forward to play with her from behind. He touched her so lightly, tantalizing her there with his fingertips, fluttering against every nerve in the region.

He gave a rumble of contentment as she gasped raggedly and then pushed herself against him, gyrating helplessly, wet again with want.

Her skirt was bunched up around her waist, and the fabric of her loose camisole grazed her nipples when Dan's hands weren't. She wanted him inside her. "Please," she whispered. "Please."

She clung to the newel post as he fished out another condom from his nearby pants and then obliged her, taking her inch by inch from behind. She arched her back and pushed against him, craving that complete fullness of before. Once he was sheathed fully, he pulled almost all the way out before driving in hard. He set a more rapid tempo this time, sliding in and out of her like a well-oiled piston, driving her crazy with each stroke.

He began to play her with his fingers again in front, and the combination of pleasures overwhelmed her. She tensed and climbed up, up, up—then exploded without warning into a million particles of light.

Dan drove into her furiously in a shorter, more staccato rhythm and then erupted into soft curses behind her before stiffening and driving home one last, quivering time.

Lil noticed that he, too, was now hanging on to the newel post. They stayed that way for a minute or so, unable to move, until Nana's grandfather clock sounded twelve sonorous chimes in succession.

The stroke of midnight reminded her of Cinderella at the ball. Would her sexy siren self just disappear now?

9

DAN DROVE BACK to his hotel with the Mustang's top down and the Connecticut wind in his hair. What in the Sam Hill had gotten into Miss Manners?

Whatever it was, he liked it. He'd greatly enjoyed teaching her all the basics of Uncivilization 101. Well, all the basics that he could pack into one short evening. And it made him feel better, somehow, about knuckling under to the standards and expectations of Lovely Nigel and his mother.

You're doing it for Claire. He reminded himself of that again, but he knew better. The reality of the situation was that it was Bloody Nigel and Mama who had instilled Claire with their snotty values and beliefs. They'd molded her into a proper upper crust young English girl. So unfortunately it was their standards that he was conforming to. But he'd be damned to hell and back again if they could find anything to criticize about his behavior at this wedding. He had something to prove: that not only was he as good as them, but he could outplay them at their own game. They'd left behind an inconvenient, sullen fourteen-year-old. By God he'd show them that he was now a man to be reckoned with.

His lip curled. And now Claire probably had turned into a snob, just like them. A cucumber-sandwich nibbling priss-pot. Sodding Nigel would be so proud.

Dan accelerated onto the highway, which was laughably narrow and confined compared to any road in Texas. *Lilia's a priss-pot. But a very nice and sexy one.* At least on the surface.

He shrugged off the thought, happier to wallow in his stereotypes. And he had a good laugh at the process that Bloody Nigel must have gone through to "civilize" Mama properly. Dan was quite sure the man hadn't taken her anywhere in public for at least a year, not trusting her to behave properly and not make a laughingstock out of him in front of his English cronies.

How sad. Yet Dan was equally sure that Mama had been an eager pupil, soaking up all the nuances of the British class structure like a sponge. Sadder still: the people at the top, the ones she wanted so badly to impress, would always whisper behind her back, always snub her—simply because she was American and had been working class. Hell, they'd snub Lovely Nigel, too—because he'd worked for his money.

England wasn't the U.S., where anyone could better himself and society was somewhat fluid.

Dan's thoughts went back to Lilia. Had she ever had good sex before? He doubted it. She'd been too shocked—and yet delighted. There'd been an innocence to her that didn't go with her air of worldly sophistication.

If he were a gambling man, he'd lay odds on the probability that Miz Lil had previously only experienced the missionary position, on a mattress with the lights out.

He grinned. He was pretty sure that he'd rocked her world, flipping up her skirt like that and ripping off her panty hose and eating her right on the table. She'd behaved like a lady who'd never been partaken of. Was that possible in this day and age? If so, he planned to have even more fun with her.

Dan went hard again just at the thought of that sweet little mons, the bite-size little breasts that responded to the slightest flick of his tongue and the raw, throaty sounds she'd made. Miz Lilia might have started off the evening a lady…but she sure hadn't ended it that way.

Suddenly Dan felt somewhat ashamed.

Why? She asked you to do it. She damn near sent you an engraved invitation. She begged for it, even if it was in that unbelievably repressed way of hers.

But he couldn't shake the feeling that he'd somehow defiled her, sullied her purity by putting his big, dirty country hands on her and making her scream for mercy.

Screw manners? Yeah, he'd screwed 'em, all right.

What was it about Lilia that turned him on? She wasn't his normal type. He was all about lush-bodied, all-American babes in tight jeans, not tiny, small-breasted exotics in prim suits.

Had his sexual desire for her risen out of hostility and the urge to rip the fabric of social perfection? Troubling thought. Or had it simply been the natural response of a man invited to seduce a woman?

Dan told himself that any red-blooded man in his

place would have responded the way he had. She'd offered sex. He'd taken her up on it. End of story.

He arrived at the hotel, parked his car, put the top up. The room was just as bland as it had been last night: blue and beige and faux-cozy in an institutional way. He pitched the three-ring etiquette binder off the bed, shucked off his clothes and fell facedown on it, still able to feel the pressure of Lil's small heels on his bare back.

LIL DROVE to the office next morning after a terrible night's sleep, caught up in dreams which alternated between fantasy and nightmare. Talk about fark lessons! She'd given Dan some, and he'd given her some. Funny how both involved prongs and healthy appetites. Ahem.

On the one hand, her body was more relaxed than it had been in years. On the other hand, her mind was full of guilt and self-recrimination. Nana's dining room table, of all places. And Nana's foyer! What if a neighbor had come along and peeked through the small fan window at the top of the door? Come to think of it, how could she be sure that nobody had? She'd been facing the stairs, after all…. Lil closed her eyes, which was a dangerous thing to do in the morning rush hour traffic.

What was she going to say to Dan Granger this morning? "Thanks for the fark lessons, cowboy?"

And what if Shannon could somehow tell what they'd been up to? Shan was far, far too good at reading body language. Lil shuddered. Then she tried to think of a way to get back at her friend for putting the carrot juice on her desk yesterday morning. The nerve!

The idea came to her with perfect timing: the local Stop n' Shop was visible on the right. Lil pulled into the parking lot, hopped out of her Camry and headed for the diet aisle. She came out within two minutes and popped back into the car with a bag of rice cakes.

Next stop: Krispy Kreme, of course. She got a half dozen fresh doughnuts straight out of the oven and the extra empty box she asked for.

Then before driving the final mile to the Finesse offices, Lil took the rice cakes out of their bag and placed them into the empty Krispy Kreme box. She covered them with a piece of bakery tissue so the deception wouldn't be discovered until Shan actually opened the box, slavering with anticipation. *Mwah ha ha ha...*

Then she called Jane on her cell phone and filled her in so she wouldn't spoil the ugly surprise. "I'll have the real ones in my office," she said. "In a file drawer."

Dan had once again beaten her to Finesse. Lil parked beside his Mustang and told the little butterflies in her stomach to fly away. She smoothed her hair and checked her lipstick. Excellent. No signs of last night's shameless hussy who'd spread her legs on the dining room table. Ugh. Had she really done that?

A most unladylike grin commandeered her mouth and flashed into the rear view mirror. Yes, indeed she had. And oh, what a ride!

Stop it. Lil ripped the uncharacteristic, renegade leer off her face and got out of the car with her two boxes and elegant handbag. She approached the glass door carefully today, her knee still bruised from Granger's attempt at chivalry yesterday morning.

There was no need for her caution: he sprawled, gently snoring, on the camel-backed reproduction sofa in the reception area, the flowered upholstery incongruous with his Western wear. He opened his eyes and yawned as she came in the door. A smile spread across his face. "Mornin', Lil. Sleep well?" And Dan winked.

A hot blush suffused her face as he zeroed in on the Krispy Kreme boxes and sat bolt upright. "Here," she said, "take this one back to my office. Ignore the one I'm putting in the kitchenette, okay? It's not what it seems."

He cocked his head at her and took the box. "Hmmmm. Okay. You gonna explain over coffee?"

She nodded.

He headed down the hall with the real doughnuts, and she took the ringers to the little kitchen, setting them on the counter. She poured two cups of coffee and followed him, waving "hi" to Jane as she passed her friend's office. Jane was on the phone but waggled her fingers at her.

Dan looked up as Lilia entered. "So what's in the other box, Lil?"

She smiled evilly. "Rice cakes. Payback to Shannon for the carrot juice yesterday."

"Yeah, what was that all about?" He looked intrigued.

"Oh. Nothing. She just knows that I, um, hate it. So did you sleep well, Dan?" She blinked, all innocence, and set his coffee in front of him on the desk.

He nodded his thanks and grabbed a doughnut. "Mmm," he said, and to her discomfort, he licked at the glossy, wet sugar on the pastry without biting it. Then he circled the inner hole with the tip of his tongue, stabbing it through a couple of times.

"Stop that!" she hissed. "You're disgusting. And my partner is across the hall."

The corners of his eyes crinkled devilishly and he showed no sign of remorse. He took a big bite of the doughnut and groaned. Once he'd swallowed it, he said, "I had a wonderful time last night, Miz Lil. Thank you for everything. Dessert was beyond incredible."

Lil heard papers rustling in Jane's office. "It was my grandmother's recipe," she said a shade too loudly.

"Oh, I seriously doubt that." He smiled.

She squinted at him in what she hoped was a menacing manner, and looked at the clock. "Bring that doughnut and your coffee with you. We've got an appointment with Jean Pierre this morning."

His smug smile disappeared. "And who, exactly, is Jean Pierre?"

"Jean Pierre's going to teach you some ballroom dancing." Lil picked up her own coffee and her keys while her client grimaced, trying to talk herself out of the calories in a doughnut. Useless. Why try? She fished one out of the box, offered Dan another, and took the remaining three in to Jane, who stuck them in her bottom drawer.

Then they headed for Jean Pierre and his business, DanceMaestro, in the picturesque little town of West Hartford.

A Parisian transplant, Jean Pierre La Croix had relocated to Connecticut to join the love of his life, Simon James, who owned the catering business that Lil had gotten the food from last night.

Jean Pierre's dance studio was located in one of the few modern buildings close to West Hartford town center, and he had a passion for all things art nouveau and art deco. The place was smothered in Erte prints, Tiffany glass and modern rugs modeled on Gustav Klimt paintings. Lil found it a bit much, and never failed to laugh at the horrendous painting by Simon which featured Jean Pierre's face on the body of a sleekly draped 1920's woman in black. She/he gazed coyly out from a red background, with cupid's bow lips and pin curls to die for.

Jean Pierre, when not modeling in dresses for paintings, looked like a peaked version of Clark Gable and stroked his waxed mustache a lot.

"Bonjour, Leelia!" he exclaimed when they walked in. He sprang out of his chair and kissed her on both cheeks while Dan gazed around the office space in bemusement.

"Bonjour, Jean. Comment allez-vous?"

"Très bien, ma cherie. Et vous?"

"Bien, merci."

"And you have brought wees you J.R. Ewing, yes? From Dallas?" He inspected Dan from head to toe, his mustache quivering like an inquisitive mouse's whiskers.

"Haaaaaaa," said Dan, looking unamused.

"'Allo, allo! Baaht, where are your spurs?" Jean Pierre threw up his hands and looked at Lilia. "You want I should teach zis man ze waltz? He is more for, how you say? Ze sheet-keeker dance."

Dan's expression got darker. "You callin' me a shit-kicker, you little frog?"

"*Oui,* ze keeking of ze merde! Ze, ah, Cotton-Eyed Jean? Line dance?"

Lil intervened. "Dan, he is fascinated by Texas culture—"

Granger stared down from his superior height at the little Frenchman. "Cotton-eyed *Joe,* froggy."

"Yes! Yes!" Jean stuck out his arms and embraced two imaginary friends on either side of him. Then he began to hum and skip, doing some Western abomination of the cancan. "Yee ha, la la la!"

Dan burst out laughing, to Lil's relief. "Where the hell did you find this idi—uh, guy?"

"Yee ha, la la la!" Jean Pierre galloped around the room in a circle.

"By reputation. He's very good."

"Not at line-dancing, he ain't." Dan shook his head.

"Try to remember to say 'isn't.'"

"Yeah, whatever."

"Well, if he's so bad, why don't you show him how it's done?" Lilia challenged Dan.

His response was a snort. "Are you kiddin'? I'm not snugglin' up with that guy."

"Then how on earth do you think he's going to teach you to waltz or to fox-trot? You'll be holding hands with him soon enough."

Dan looked horrified.

Jean Pierre completed his circle of the room and clapped for himself. *"Oui! C'est bien!"*

"C'est sucked," muttered Dan under his breath.

Lilia ignored him and turned to Jean-Pierre. "Dan will be attending a formal English wedding, Jean, and—"

"Pah!" Jean Pierre spat. "Ze English."

Dan brightened. "You don't like 'em, either, eh?"

Jean rolled his Gallic eyes. "Zey are smug, zey are fat, zey are repressed. And ze English food! Pah! *Horrible!*"

"I'm changin' my mind about you, Froggy. I think we might get along."

"Now, gentlemen," said Lil. "I have wonderful English friends. These are gross generalizations and you should not take them to heart."

Dan snorted. "You ever need a reason to hate the English, I'll introduce you to Lovely Sodding Nigel, my stepfather. You'll be rushing to generalize in no time, I promise."

"As I was saying—" Lil ignored him and turned to Jean "—Dan needs to learn some basic ballroom steps. He should be smooth and not step on any toes. He needs to be able to lead a lady confidently, in front of a crowd. I imagine he'll be dancing with his sister, the bride."

Jean pursed his lips and walked around Dan as if he were a 4-H prize goat. *"Oui.* You will get J.R. some, ah, choes? Ze sheet-keekers, *non.* Not so good for dancing."

"Boots are fan-friggin'-tastic for dancin', froggy."

"You vil not call me zis 'froggy.'"

"Then you *vil* not call me J.R. Got it?"

The two men eyed each other appraisingly. *"C'est*

bien," declared Jean Pierre. He leaped toward Dan and grabbed his hand. Then he clasped him around the waist and pulled him close. Dan stiffened like a maiden broomstick.

To Lilia, Jean said, "Be still mine heart. He ees 'ot, he ees buff. If I were not spoken for, and eef he did not wear so 'orrible a belt, I would 'ave him. Oh, yes, indeed."

"The hell you would!" Dan growled and sent him flying. Luckily for Jean Pierre, he was agile and so he didn't crash into the wall.

"What is meaning of zis? Brute!"

"I'm not touching that guy," Granger said to Lil.

"Dan, he's harmless!"

"Zis J.R., he ees violent, Leelia!"

"Jean, behave. You did provoke him."

"He ees not…gay?"

"No, he is *not!*" Dan thundered.

Lilia rushed to explain. "Listen, Dan, in Paris it's really only the gay men who work out, who have muscle like you. He just assumed—"

"Last time I checked, we were not in friggin' Paris!"

"Everyone, *calm down*. We are here for a simple dancing lesson. Nothing more, nothing less. Now, can we get on with things, gentlemen?"

"I am not gettin' snuggly with that man," Dan said.

Lilia threw up her hands. "Fine. Then *I'll* dance with you. Jean will direct us both. All right?"

Some of Dan's anger dissipated and a gleam appeared in his eye. "Now that," he said, "works real well for me." He walked over to her, took her hand and pulled her against him, glaring at Jean.

His big silver belt buckle was cold through her blouse, but Lil's stomach flipped and the butterflies returned. Little electric shocks zipped through her body.

Dan made a very male sound of satisfaction.

Jean Pierre sighed and pulled at his waxed mustache. "*Quel tragedie.* No, Beeg Tex is not gay. *Alors,* we waltz."

10

As THEY LEFT the dance studio, Dan congratulated himself on not having punted the little frog through his fussy stained-glass window and into Main Street traffic below.

"See, that wasn't so bad, now was it?" Miz Lilia said to him as he opened the passenger door of the Mustang for her.

He snorted.

"That's not the sort of noise a gentleman makes, Dan. The polite response is, 'no, not at all.' Graceful and noncommittal."

"And another whopper! That man *touched* me, Lilia."

"Oh, please. He hardly had a chance to bounce off your belt buckle before you tossed him into the wall! Which, by the way, is not at all polite, either."

"You don't say."

"And he apologized before we left."

Dan snorted again. "The man was staring at my *crotch* when he said 'no, ah, hard feelinks, eh?' You call that an apology?"

Lil pressed her lips together to keep from laughing. "He was mourning."

Dan stared at her incredulously before speeding out of the parking lot. "Miz Lil, you are not as innocent as you let on, and I ain't goin' back there."

She sighed. "Unfortunately I am, and you are. Going back there," she clarified. "You have to learn to dance, Dan."

His jaw worked. Then he shot her a sideways, calculating glance. "I'll go back there if you'll spend the night with me."

"Dan!"

"That's the deal. Take it or leave it."

"I'll think about it. Now, take a left at the next street. We're going to see Enrique for your haircut at eleven."

Dan frowned at the car's digital clock. "It's eleven-fifteen."

"Enrique's always late. He's an artiste and cannot be rushed."

Dan groaned. "Oh, no. What are you going to put me through now?"

"Enrique is marvelous."

"Uh-huh. Does Marvelous Enrique lead an alternative lifestyle, too?"

"Enrique is married with three beautiful children. Don't stereotype, Dan. It's rude and displays a narrow mind."

"Oh, puleeeze. I just call it like I see it."

"Then you haven't seen nearly enough, now have you?"

She was starting to piss him off again with that superior socialite tone of hers. He'd had enough of that from Mama over the years since her transformation. He decided to knock Lil off her ivory pedestal again. "I haven't seen *nearly enough* of you nekkid."

Predictably she blushed. "Take the next right, Dan."

"I'd rather take you, darlin'."

"Dan, stop it!"

"All lights were green for 'go' last night. What's the matter, honey, have you replaced me already?"

"What? No! What do you think, that I'm some kind of…of…slut?"

"Hey, sluts have all the fun, hon. Besides, I'm teasing you. I don't think you could pick up a man to save your life." He grinned.

Obviously stung, she said, "I could, too. I'm just not in the habit of doing so."

"You say it like you think it's a bad habit. Spend the night with me, Lil. I got all kinds of bad habits to teach you in Uncivilization 101."

"Here we are," she said in false, bright tones.

"Come get nasty with me, nice girl."

She bolted out of the car without waiting for him to open her door.

Dan smiled and went after her.

THE SALON was draped in a lot of toilet-cleaner-blue velvet and cluttered with gold frames. This Enrique guy obviously thought he was royalty, since he even had a big vase stuffed full of peacock feathers. Dan winced and looked for a place that a self-respecting man could sit down.

Even the receptionist wore blue eye shadow and blue

nail polish and her face had gold sprinkles on it. She looked like a harem girl.

He cast an uneasy glance at Lilia and adjusted himself.

Her eyes widened. "Never, never, never do that in public again!" she snapped.

"What? Damn, it was torqued wrong."

"I don't care if it's tied in a knot, you wait until you're in private to do that." Lilia shook her head and looked as shocked as if he had just tried to murder someone. Did the woman need to relax, or what?

After a ten-minute wait, this Enrique clown danced out to meet them, and Dan knew immediately that he was in trouble again.

Enrique looked like a pint-size Ricky Ricardo. He kissed Lilia and beamed at her. "Allo, beeeyoootiful!"

"Hi, handsome." Lil dimpled.

The little guy clapped his hand to his chest. "She steal my heart," he announced, to no one in particular. "It make boom-boom!" Then he looked at Dan. "Where you lasso thees one? Who butcher your hair, Cowboy? And the belt buckle? I could use for mirror!"

What the hell? Nobody seemed to like his belt, and this was getting old. Dan folded his arms across his chest and glowered at the man. "Aren't you guys supposed to suck up to your customers, instead of insulting them? And my dad cuts my hair, thank you very much."

"He use hedge-trimmer? He is blind, no?" Enrique grinned unapologetically and poked him in the belly.

"Ow! What the hell?"

"You seet in my chair, Cowboy. We transform you

into the prince. The boots," he said to Lilia, "the boots I like, but no the belt. You burn, eh? And the shirt, too. He got good face, good…how you say? Ah, build. He talk a leetle funny." Enrique draped Dan in a navy-blue plastic cape and began to hum tunelessly.

"Excuse me, but I *am* in the room, you little tamale."

Lilia cringed, but Enrique burst out laughing. "Tamale? No, no. I wear no corn husk." He fished around in a drawer and came out with some wicked looking scissors and a comb. Clutching these in one hand, he reached for a spray bottle with the other. "You are late, so you no get hair wash."

Dan's mouth dropped open. "Of all the—we were *not* late! Well, we were, but *you* were late."

Enrique ignored this, sprayed him with the water, set down the sprayer again and grabbed him by the hair. *Snip! Snip! Snip!*

"You're enjoying this," Dan accused Lilia.

She nodded and smiled serenely. Then her cell phone rang. "Excuse me."

She pulled it from her purse, which matched her shoes. He half expected her to pull out a pair of kid gloves in the same shade. "Hello?"

As Dan watched she turned pink and looked pleased. "Serves you right," she said. "Besides, rice cakes have lots of fiber in them, and you're full of it."

Had Miss Manners just insulted her blond Amazon partner? Well, Dan was all for it, since the wench had taken his suitcases to the Salvation Army.

"What do you mean, revenge? I just took revenge on

you, for the carrot juice! The cycle should end there....
Oh, well, fine. I'm trembling.... Be quiet and go and get
Mr. Granger a couple of new belts. He'll also need a
raincoat and some riding gear—"

"No pansy pants!" Dan growled.

"—yes, bring the boots, too, and we'll hope that
he doesn't need special fitting. There's no time for
custom-made ones...but the boots are the most important, since he'll need them for his riding lesson tomorrow. He swears he won't wear the hat, but bring
that as well."

Enrique continued to snip and Dan wondered if he
was leaving him any hair at all. He decided it was best
to close his eyes.

"I don't need a riding lesson," he announced to Lilia
when she got off the phone.

"We had this talk. Just do one and then we'll reeval-
uate if you still don't think it's necessary."

Dan sighed and Enrique distracted him by pulling
here and there on his hair like a monkey and cutting more
off with a different pair of scissors, "For texture, yes?"

Yeah, whatever.

Finally the little dude dusted him with a gigantic
blue powder puff and sprayed a tennis-ball sized blob
of white foam into his hands. Then he clapped them
onto Dan's head and worked in the nasty goo. He
whipped out a hair-dryer and brandished it like a gun,
pointing it, pretending to sight his target through the
back, and pulling the "trigger."

He freeze-dried Dan's hair into fashionable swirls

and spikes and then sprayed it with some kind of aerosol glue. *"Bueno!"* he finally declared, whipping off the blue cape.

Dan stared at himself and put a hand up to touch the miracle, only to have the hand smacked by Enrique.

"No poking the masterpiss, eh? Thees is work of art. Enrique is great genius."

"Touch me again, Tamale, and I'll gut you. Understand?"

Enrique turned to Lilia, his hands on his hips. "He is rude, this one. He like his hair? You like?"

"Yes, he like his hair," Dan growled.

"Enrique, you've outdone yourself. He looks like a movie star!"

"Yes, yes! He is…ahm…what his name, eh? He is the Nick Lachey? But lighter hairs and eyes."

"And no Jessica," Lil said dryly.

"Yeah," Dan waggled his brows lecherously, "but I've got—"

He broke off at a bona fide glare from Miss Manners.

"You have many womens, yes?" Enrique asked. "Eh, you will have many mores without the belt."

"Enough about my belt!" Dan said. "And no, I don't have many women. I like 'em one at a time. It'd be nice to keep one around for a while, but I can't seem to find one willing to live on a ranch in the middle of nowhere. Plus the selection at your average agricultural convention is limited."

"Agricultural convention?" Lilia raised her brows.

"Yes. I'm in the ranching business. Got my MBA

from Texas A & M, darlin'. You look surprised. Did you think I'd never graduated fifth grade?"

"Of course I didn't think that, Dan." But she was stunned to find that he had an MBA. He was more educated than she.

Enrique flapped the cape at them. "You go now. I have other appointment. *Muchas gracias!*"

Dan exchanged a glance with Lil as he got out of the chair. "Thank you, Enrique. I'll be sure to order you a belt just like mine and ship it to you C.O.D."

"WHERE TO NOW, Lil?" Dan asked later that evening. They had just finished dinner at an elegant restaurant in Greenwich. He'd learned a hundred more stupid social rules and he was heartily tired of being corrected on everything from his grammar to his conversation to his posture.

She'd made him lose his normal clothing that afternoon, dressed him in khakis and a blue blazer and hauled his ass to high tea at some swank hotel, where he'd been a lot more interested in the possibility of hourly rates than teeny little sandwiches that wouldn't satisfy a bird. At least he hadn't smashed any china or destroyed any furniture.

Then, to add insult to injury, she'd made him change again—this time into a friggin' suit—and drive an hour for dinner in the snottiest part of Connecticut.

Dinner had been fabulous, but he wasn't about to admit that to Lil.

She yawned delicately behind her fine-boned hand. "I'm ready for bed."

"Excellent. I am so glad to hear that," Dan said with a grin. *Finally! Something fun.*

She looked startled. "I didn't mean it like *that*."

"You said you'd consider spending the night with me."

"Dan, I really shouldn't do that."

"Why the hell not? I tell a real good bedtime story. I give a great back rub. And the Granger Shower Hour is without equal."

"Dan…"

They'd reached the Mustang now, which looked odd in the lot of the chateaulike restaurant and inn. The place was peppered with Mercedes Benzes and Jaguars and BMWs. Dan's bright red rental car stood out like a sore thumb—a cheap one. Which made him laugh, considering the fact that he could probably buy the place twice over and still have money to redecorate. He might have rough manners, but he did well for himself.

"Yes, Lil?"

"We have to work together. And I shouldn't have been so…forward last night. I'm embarrassed."

Her dark eyes slid away from his and her adorable, prim, pink mouth pursed. "Lil, you got nothing to be embarrassed about. You said you were tired of living like a little old lady, right?"

She nodded.

"Your nana brought you up, all by herself? And you were a nice girl, never got into any trouble, huh?"

She nodded again.

"Well, I'd say it's high time that you got naughty. And

Get FREE BOOKS and a FREE GIFT when you play the...

LAS VEGAS
GAME

Just scratch off the gold box with a coin. Then check below to see the gifts you get!

YES! I have scratched off the gold box. Please send me my 2 **FREE BOOKS** and **gift for which I qualify.** I understand that I am under no obligation to purchase any books as explained on the back of this card.

351 HDL D7XN   151 HDL D7YP

FIRST NAME   LAST NAME

ADDRESS

APT.#   CITY

STATE/PROV.   ZIP/POSTAL CODE   (H-B-10/05)

7	7	7	Worth TWO FREE BOOKS plus a BONUS Mystery Gift!
🍒	🍒	🍒	Worth TWO FREE BOOKS!
🔔	🔔	♣	TRY AGAIN!

www.eHarlequin.com

I think the best gift I can give you is a little embarrassment, Granger-style."

He took two steps and pinned her against the side of the Mustang. He took her mouth with his and made love to it thoroughly, losing himself between her lips.

He spanned her small waist with his hands and moved upward to cup her breasts, right there in the parking area, in full view of the restaurant.

She pulled away from his mouth, gasping, and she pushed at his chest. "Stop it, Dan! Everyone can see us."

"I know." He rubbed her nipples through the simple black corset top she wore—an article of clothing that had been driving him crazy all through dinner. It was obviously expensive, made of beautiful fabric and very tasteful, in spite of the provocative lacing at the front. She wore no bra underneath, not even a strapless one.

Lil moaned, gave in to his touch for a split second, her little nipples puckering, and then pushed at him again. He didn't budge. Instead he moved his hands down to her ass and pulled her hard against his erection. "Feel that?" he whispered. "That's what you do to me, honey. You are so hot…I want to spread your legs and take you right on the hood of this car."

"Dan!" She blushed fire.

"That turns you on, doesn't it?"

"No!"

"Yeah, it does. I can see it in your eyes, Lil. And I want what's under that little black skirt of yours."

He moved one hand down to the hem of her skirt and crept under it.

"Get out of—" She slapped at his hand. "Stop it!"

"I want to part your sweet knees and look at you there." He stroked her thigh, moved his fingers up under her panties and felt her wet, quivering female flesh.

She mewled.

"I want to eat you out until you scream."

"Oh my God! You can't say things like—"

He rubbed her clitoris and then slid a finger into her. "So sweet, so juicy. You wanna feel my mouth there, Lil?"

She covered her ears. "Stop it!" But she didn't close her knees, didn't shove him seriously.

He grinned, withdrew his hand from her skirt and pulled her hands down, putting them on his cock. Then he whispered into her naked ear again. "I want you even wetter. I want you wild. I want to make you come so hard you see stars."

He was so busy whispering that he didn't hear the white-jacketed restaurant employee until he cleared his throat behind them. "Sir? Madam? I do regret this, but we have to ask you to leave."

Horrified, poor Lil dived under his suit jacket and refused to show her face.

"I understand," Dan said. "We just got a little carried away. Come on, honey." He opened the car door and Lil slunk inside, her face hidden by her hands and her beautiful black hair. She was shaking.

Dan got into the car himself, waved adios to the waiter and drove them out of there.

He looked down at Lil's bent head and chuckled.

She bolted upright. "Are you *laughing,* you son of a bi—?"

"Did you just almost cuss at me, Miss Manners?"

"Yes! I can never, ever go back there, now! They *know* me. And if this gets out, my professional reputation is *ruined.*"

11

DAN LAUGHED AGAIN, to Lil's fury. Then he asked, "Why?"

Was the man really that thick? "Are you honestly asking me that question? Do I have to spell it out? Because an etiquette consultant does not do such things in front of an audience!"

"Lil, be reasonable. Who really knows you there?"

"The owner! I've met him socially."

"And was he around tonight?"

She bit her lip. "No. He's the chef. He was in the kitchen."

"And I paid the bill with my credit card. So unless you're cozy with the waitstaff or other dinner guests, there's really no damage done to your professional reputation."

"I still can't go back there! What if someone recognizes me?"

Dan sighed. "I think you're being paranoid. Do you want to stop living like a little old lady? Or do you want to beat yourself up over the way you might look to a bunch of people you don't know?"

Lil clenched her hands in her lap and stared out the

window. "No, I want to beat *you* up over the way I might look to those people."

"Oh, so it's my fault."

"Yes! *You* touched my breasts. *You* put your hand up my skirt. *You* talked dirty to me."

"And *you* enjoyed it. *You* didn't knee me in the balls. So where does that leave us, besides sexually frustrated? I don't know about you, but I've got such a hard-on I can practically hit the gas pedal with it."

Lil choked. "Well, I'm sorry but I don't know what to do about that."

"I do." Dan pulled the car off the road and headed toward some woods.

"What are you doing?"

"You ever go parking back in high school, Lil? Or were you too busy wearing white stockings and perfecting your French?"

"Dan, take me home."

He stopped the car. "If that's what you really want, then of course I'll drive you back. But you do have unfinished homework for Uncivilization 101, darlin'."

She swallowed, hating that she still wanted him even though she'd like to kill him.

"See, on page forty-three of the text, the assignment is to take off those panties that were gettin' in my way."

She took a deep breath and tried to fight the desire that lapped at her along with his voice.

"You always do your homework, don't you, Lil? And there's nobody around to see. You afraid to shock an owl or something, sweetheart?"

She expelled the breath and found that her thighs were trembling.

"Still wet for me, honey?"

His teeth gleamed white in the darkness and a shaft of moonlight bathed his strong forearm, highlighting the corded muscle. Electricity shot through her stomach at the sight. She licked her lips.

"Take them off. Just for me."

She'd lost her mind before and the damage was done. She might as well lose her panties. Blocking out the censorious voices in her head, Lil met his gaze. Then she lifted her hips, slid her hand up under her skirt and hooked a finger into the elastic of her underwear.

His breathing came faster and his lips parted.

She tugged the panties over her hips, down her thighs until they rested at her knees. Pale blue silk, they, too, caught the moonlight.

Dan hit the gas and the car shot forward, slowing as they reached the trees. He crept into them and killed the lights, then the engine.

The only sounds around them were those of little night insects, the wind in the trees and their breathing.

Dan turned to her. "There's a lever on the side of your seat. Ease it back."

Lil did so, her panties still circling her knees. He leaned forward and pulled them down over her calves and ankles, then finally over her feet as she lifted one for him and then the other.

"No stockings," he whispered. "Just beautiful, bare skin." He threw the panties into the back seat. "I've never wanted anyone as bad as I want you, Lil. You're killing me. You tell me, 'wear this jacket, don't say that word. Put your napkin here, bring a hostess gift there.' And the whole time you're lecturing me, all I want to do is—" he pushed up her top "this." He fastened his mouth around a nipple and she half moaned, half gasped. "And this." He moved to the other breast, suckling it. "And this." He moved his fingers between her thighs and stroked her with the tips.

"Oh…"

He fluttered them against her and rubbed his middle finger along her folds until he found her clit, which he rubbed in circles until she whimpered, raised her hips and arched her back shamelessly.

Nothing in her life had ever felt this good. This man had an extraordinary sexual power over her that she couldn't fight. He held all the mystery of chemistry in his magical hands and mouth, and she was desperate to feel him inside her again.

"Please, Dan…"

"Please, what?"

She couldn't vocalize it.

"What do you want, honey? You gotta tell me. You want my mouth, my hands or my cock?"

How did she say it?

"Talk to me, baby."

"I want…you."

"Inside?"

She nodded, feeling a blush spread over her from head to toe.

Dan got out of the car. Where was he going? He slammed the driver's side door and rounded the hood, then opened her door and unbuckled his belt. Just the sounds of him undressing turned her on, quickened her breath with anticipation. "Let me sit there." He stretched out a hand to her and she got out, switched places with him.

Dan sat on the edge of the seat and drew her onto his knees, pushing her skirt up around her waist. He tugged her forward and rubbed her with his penis until she thought she'd come apart right then, the cool air on her backside and his hot erection under her.

Then he parted her and drove slickly home in one thrust, gripping her bottom hard.

Lil cried out with the pleasure of it, the sudden fullness, the hot streak of lightning that shot through her.

He groaned against her neck and then took her mouth with his, moving her up and down on him, thrusting as if his life depended on it.

She gripped his shoulders, digging her fingers into the muscle, scraping her nipples along the shirt he hadn't bothered to take off. Her camisole was still on, too, but bunched up under her arms.

Dan bent her back, still thrusting, and took one of her breasts into his mouth, rolling the taut peak against his tongue and sucking her into an altered state where the only focus she had was the indescribable sensations between her legs.

She could feel his cock almost all the way up to her throat, and it penetrated some bubble of tension she didn't even know she had, bursting it into a channel of bliss. Then the small narrow channel filled with hot honey, which rose and rose until it spilled over and drenched her in a thick, sweet climax very different from any she'd had last night—but just as satisfying.

Dan had slowed his tempo and he drove home between her legs one, two, three more times before shuddering and spilling himself inside her. "Aaaahhhhhh," he groaned into her hair.

They still held each other so tightly that breathing was difficult, and Lil forced herself to peel her fingers off his shoulders. "I don't know what it is you do to me, or how you do it," she whispered. "But you make me feel so good. I'm not a lady around you. But I sure am a woman."

"COME SLEEP WITH ME, Lilia." His voice was hoarsely sexy as he drove them back the forty-five miles or so to Farmington.

"I don't have a change of clothes, or even a toothbrush."

"So? I don't plan on letting you sleep in your clothes, and you can brush your teeth in the morning when I take you home."

"Dan…"

"Just say yes. Tell me that if you don't come back to my hotel with me, you won't sleep a wink for thinking about my hands on you all night. My mouth on you. Me inside you."

"How many times can a person do it in one night? You're a goat, Dan."

He grinned. "Just call me Billy. Call me anything. Just come back to my room with me."

"I really shouldn't."

"Should, darlin', is a useless word. You either do or you don't, but screw whether you should. It's second-guessing and all it does is make you feel guilty. Nothing about sex should make you feel guilty. You're not married or engaged or a whore. Now come on, I'm not done uncivilizing you, yet."

"How can I turn you down when you put it that way?" Lil raised an eyebrow at him.

"Yes!" he pumped a fist into the air, and she couldn't help but laugh. He was like a teenage boy who'd just scored a goal.

She pondered the dualities in his character. He was a man who didn't, in general, give a damn what anybody thought—yet here he was, putting himself through the equivalent of charm school so that he wouldn't embarrass his little sister at her wedding.

He obviously hated all of Lil's rules, but he soaked them up like a sponge. And he thought she was prissy and formal, yet he couldn't seem to get enough of her. What did it all mean?

And what was it in her that responded so completely to his sexuality and his rough manners? She wasn't the type to fall for a man like him. But she thrilled to his simple masculinity and his quirky, cynical way of looking at the world. His sureness of self. The fact that he seemed to understand where she came from, even though they were from two different planets. He came from a raw, all-male one, she from a refined all-female one.

She didn't have the answers, but she did have a fling.

While she hoped that Nana wouldn't be horrified and ashamed of her for going to spend a torrid night twisting in the sheets with a client, Lil felt that if she didn't, she'd be letting some part of herself down.

She'd always sought to please Nana and her standards, deserve the love that Lisbeth had shown her. But Nana was gone now…wasn't it time to please herself?

Before Lil knew it, they were pulling into the parking lot of a big chain hotel. God, she couldn't walk in there with no panties on! She turned and felt behind her for the missing blue scrap of silk, but came up with nothing. She unfastened her seat belt and turned, now on her knees.

"Don't you dare," murmured Dan, undoing his seat belt, too. He slipped a hand up under her skirt and stroked her bare buttocks. "We have no use for those."

"But…"

"Butt," he agreed. "Very nice butt. Come on, Miz Lilia. You think anybody working the desk in there has X-ray vision? I doubt it." He got out and opened her door, held his big hand out to her.

She put her small one into it and let him help her out. They walked into the hotel without incident, rode the elevator to his floor and entered a room like any other hotel room she'd been in.

The difference was that Dan was here, Dan who in a split second had no shirt and pulled her against his lightly furred, spectacularly muscular chest. Just the sight of it made her knees go weak, but the feel of it…the rough hair against her cheek, his nipples under her tongue, the rich, salty taste of his skin.

She bit lightly at his nipples and he groaned, closing his eyes. She really had no idea what to do next, so she just followed her instincts. She sank her teeth into his pecs and then alternately kissed them. She ran her tongue down between them until she got to the strip of hair at his belly. Pausing, she closed her eyes and thought of carrots. She could do this. She wanted to give him pleasure as he'd given it to her.

And, okay—she wanted, for the first time in her life, the sexual power that he'd had over her. Could she make him writhe and buck and tangle his hands in her hair, too? Could she make him beg for release as she had? She was going to find out.

Lil knelt before him and cupped him with her hand through his suit trousers. She'd known he would be hard already, and he didn't disappoint her.

Dan sucked in a breath and looked down with something akin to disbelief as she unzipped him and put her hand inside his pants, stroking him through the thin cotton boxers he wore, then parting those and pulling him out so that he sprang free. She caressed the velvety skin of his penis, fascinated by the head and the single translucent drop that had formed at the eye.

She cast a look upward at him to find him looking stunned as she moved her mouth close to the tip of him. His breathing was ragged and he'd taken his lower lip between his teeth. Sweat beaded above his mouth.

Lil bent her head and, drawn to the drop of moisture, touched the tip of her tongue to it.

"Ohhh."

The taste was peculiar but not bad, not salty as she'd heard other women claim. She slicked her tongue over the entire head of his penis and then closed her lips on it. She slid her hands around to his backside and took him by the buttocks.

Dan, cocky, more-than-masculine Dan, shook in the legs. And she was the reason. She was causing this reaction. She smiled and slid him farther into her mouth.

"Aaahhhh." His voice actually broke, and he gasped for air, sliding his hands into her hair and shaking some more.

She took him in as far as she could and then fisted one hand around the root of him, as Shannon had shown her so ridiculously on the carrot. She used the moisture from her mouth to wet her fist as she withdrew and then took him deep into her mouth again.

His breath was coming in ragged gasps now, and she rubbed underneath the root with her thumb as she started the rhythm that would please him. Then she caressed his balls with her other hand.

"I can't believe you're doing this," he moaned, moving his own hands to her cheeks. "I never thought—ooohhhhhh—you'd want to."

She sucked him firmly, and though her jaw began to ache, she enjoyed the feel of him in her mouth and the increasingly guttural noises he began to make as she took him higher and higher to the place he wanted to be.

In and out. In and out. In and out.

What was she going to do when the time came? She vaguely remembered Shannon teasing her about this, too. Lil didn't know. Was it disgusting, or was it perfectly natural?

"I'm losing it," he gasped. "I'm going to come, honey, you're killing me. I don't want to choke you, I'm gonna pull out—"

Even in the blindness of passion, her rough cowboy was a true gentleman. Lil's heart turned over as she continued to slide her fist over him and he jerked and spasmed uncontrollably.

His seed spilled between her fingers and she didn't find it disgusting. It was part of him, an expression of the pleasure she'd brought him.

"You're amazing," he whispered, as she pressed her face into his thigh and inhaled the scent of expensive wool.

Was she amazing? Really? On her first time? She'd never been tempted to do it for Li. Not once. But Dan Granger was different. And once again, she'd left her lady persona behind in order to find the woman inside her. A woman of appetites she'd never suspected.

12

SHE AWOKE NAKED in bed with him, her head pillowed on his warm, furry chest. He smelled wonderful: of male skin, something piney, tinges of laundry detergent and a waft of sporty deodorant.

She blinked the night's blur from her eyes but didn't move.

"That tickles," he complained sleepily. He opened his own eyes and looked at her. "You have the longest lashes I've ever seen. Gorgeous, but ticklish against a man's bare skin."

"Sorry."

"Don't apologize. It's a very nice way to be woken up." He stroked a hand over her hair, sending delicious shivers through her scalp. Then he moved to her neck and back, and she almost purred. His touch on her…it was heaven. Now his hand cupped her buttocks, rubbed over them, began to inch between her legs.

His fingers fluttered against her mons, his palm still nudged firmly against her backside, and it felt incredibly erotic as he played with her. Lil moaned and raised her bottom shamelessly to give him better access.

"Will you do something for me, Lilia?"

Lost to lust, she nodded without reservations.

"Okay, then. Come 'ere." He pulled her up onto his chest so she straddled it, but when she tried to lower herself onto him, he cupped her bottom and hauled her all the way up to his neck. "I want you to sit on my face."

She blinked at him in shock. "You what?"

"You heard me. Come on, darlin'. Sit right here." He pointed to his mouth.

She stayed right where she was, frozen. Then she shook her head. "I can't do that."

"Why not?"

"I just can't. It's too...dirty."

He laughed. "What's the difference between you sittin' here and me goin' down on you?"

"It's just different." She swung her leg over him and backed off the bed, still tingling from his fingers but alarmed at where he was trying to take her. She crossed one arm over her breasts and the other over her sex.

She had to draw a line somewhere. She didn't know this man well at all. He was a client. He was taking advantage of her need to walk on the wild side a little. It's not like this was turning into a relationship.

Sit on his...? Oh, no, I don't think so. That seemed to cross over from pleasurable to...to...filthy.

Dan sat up. "Where're you going?"

"I have to shower. You have to take me home. We've got a riding lesson for you in two hours."

"Come 'ere. Two hours is a long time. Let's have breakfast in bed."

She shook her head. Besides the fact that he'd

shocked her, she felt disgusting. She hadn't been able to brush her teeth last night, she hadn't washed her face, and her whole body smelled like sex. And he wanted her to…? Out of the question!

He sighed. "Do I have to come and get you?" And he started to get out of bed, too.

"No! I said no." Her legs were shaking now. "I mean it. I'm going to take a shower now. Alone."

His face was the picture of disappointment. "You are failing Uncivilization 101, Lil."

"I'm so sorry to hear that." She turned and walked into the bathroom, shut the door and turned on the water. Why did she feel like a witch? She had her boundaries.

Last night, in the darkness after a half-bottle of wine—anything had been possible. She blushed under the shower spray thinking about her mouth on his cock.

Have you ever given a blow job, Lil?

Yes. A damn fine one, thank you very much.

But you won't—

No!

Something about climbing onto a man and grinding her…her…her*self* into his face—it just didn't bear thinking about.

Then why is it making you so hot?

It's not that, it's the soap. She was soaping herself between the legs, and the stimulation was accidental, just as it was on her breasts.

They ached and her nipples were taut under the shower spray. Lil propped one leg up on the tub and let the water rinse away all the soap in various crevices. She wasn't going to touch herself anymore—that, too, was somehow dirty.

Oh, and a man's face between your legs while you're on your back isn't?

Stop it! Lil closed her eyes and focused on the one thing that would make all of this sexual torment go away: her grandmother.

She used one of the tiny bottles of shampoo, and massaged it into her hair, remembering how when she was little, Nana had carefully done this for her. She'd been so gentle, making sure not to get any in Lil's eyes.

Nana had raised her to be a nice girl. Someone with her values in the right place, and gracious manners.

It wasn't at all nice or gracious to be thinking about touching herself or riding some cowboy's dirty mouth.

And something else bothered her, too: Dan had gone straight to playing with her goodies, so to speak. He hadn't tried to kiss her on the mouth. Didn't that say something? Loud and clear?

Yes. It was a reminder that this thing between her and the cowboy was all about sex, and it had no future—which made her feel dirty all over again.

Nana would be so disappointed in her, if she knew. Before she'd died, she'd already been putting linens aside for Lil's hope chest; her wedding to Li Wong. She'd collected silver for her since she was born.

And now her granddaughter was having sex in park-ing lots and cars and hotels—and worse: on her mahogany dining table…with a man who barely knew how to use a fork.

Nice, Lilia. Very nice.

DAN TOOK ONE LOOK at the idiotic black riding boots that darling, uptight Lilia not only thought he'd pay for, but wear. "No. And I'm not wearing the velvet hat, and don't even think about the bun-hugger britches. Ain't nothin' wrong with my Western boots and a pair of jeans."

She sighed. "Dan, you may as well get used to the boots because you have to wear them in order to participate in the steeplechase the day after the wedding. The pants, too. As for the hat, that one's for the chase and offers you little protection. You'll be wearing a different one, even uglier, today. It's a safety helmet, somewhat like what bicyclists use. And yes, you will wear it, or you're not legally able to get on a horse at Central Pines Stables. It has to do with their insurance policy."

Lilia had washed any shared intimacy down the shower drain this morning, and was back to being her annoyingly polished, professional self. She behaved as if she hadn't taken him into her mouth last night, hadn't ridden him like she had in the open air on the seat of the Mustang. It really pissed him off.

She'd sat primly without speaking on the ride back to her house and given him a polite thank-you, but no kiss or any hint that she considered him anything but a tool to get her off. Was he being punished for trying to bring her pleasure?

He knew he'd shocked her, but he was damned if he understood why. Women! He guessed it was a good thing he hadn't asked her to sixty-nine with him. She would have thought he was Satan, and run screaming out of the hotel.

Dan gave the polished, black, knee-high boots another disgusted glance. "Fine. I'll put 'em on with my jeans. I'll wear the blasted helmet. But you can return those britches or put 'em through the shredder, because I'm just not the kind of guy who wears spandex. Got it?"

Her mouth tightened. "Fine. But I'll warn you that they'll feel different in the saddle than your jeans. They're slicker, and you should think about getting used to them before they cause you to break your neck over an English hedge."

He shot her an amused glance. "I haven't been unseated on a horse since I was about fifteen."

"Maybe that's because you had a nice big saddle horn to hang on to. English saddles don't have them, so good luck."

He ran his tongue over his teeth and poked it into one cheek. "I don't need your luck, Lil. And I don't appreciate you questioning my riding ability. What do you think I do all day, sweet pea?"

Hostility shimmered in the air between them, and again, he didn't understand why. Had he insulted Ms. London by asking her to do something unladylike? Well, too bad. If she was that uptight, then she was doomed to her narrow life, getting old before her time.

Or was it that she'd finished with him, now that he'd

gotten her off a few times? Had she decided, like his own mama, that he wasn't good enough for her?

The thought burned like acid in his belly. Goddamn pretentious, shallow, uptight women.

Dan sat in her fussy wing chair and eased off his Ropers. Then he wrapped the legs of his jeans around his ankles and jammed his feet into the stupid English riding boots. He was Dansy the Pansy again, for Christ's sake, and he just couldn't wait to learn how to "post" in a bloody, sodding English saddle to please bloody, sodding English Nigel and Mama and Claire.

"Fine, let's get this over with," he growled at Lilia. She followed him as he stomped out of her office and out to the Mustang.

Was that a snort he heard, coming from the evil blond Amazon's office?

AT CENTRAL PINES Stables, a pleasant, green farm outside Avon, Dan swung himself into the ridiculously small saddle on a seventeen-hand gelding named Tricks. The instructor was a middle-aged woman with graying hair named Dorothy, who showed him how to hold the reins English style: one in each hand instead of both in one hand.

The saddle just felt plain weird. But he could actually feel the horse between his legs instead of just a lot of leather and blanket.

"Don't kick Tricks to urge him forward," Dorothy warned. "He'll take off like a bat out of hell. Remember, you're going to gently squeeze with your calves when you want to urge him on. You don't need a crop with him—he doesn't like them and won't respond well."

Dan nodded and walked Tricks along side her until they got to a covered riding ring with a floor of sand.

"I understand that you're an experienced horseman," Dorothy continued.

"Yeah."

"But to ride English style, we're going to do some things differently. First, we'll teach you how to post."

Dan grimaced. The only way to live through this was to think about all the kids he'd give real riding lessons to next summer. He might be forced to the dark side for now, but he'd get his revenge. None of his boys would post or sit in a sissy English saddle.

"Then we'll warm up a little more and start taking some small fences." She looked at him. "Jumps," she clarified. "We'll start with that little in-and-out over there. Remember that you'll lean forward in the saddle, poised over the horse's withers.

"You're going to move your hands forward on Tricks' neck and do *not* pop him in the mouth when you take the jump. In other words, don't yank back on the reins in reflex. Keep your hands steady and easy, move with him as he jumps. Okay?"

"Yep."

"Go ahead and trot him around the ring, then. And post. By that I mean get your heels down in the stirrups. Then, using both your knees and your feet in the stir-rups, raise your seat with every other step, then sit. You'll get the feel for it. Pelvis forward, then back.

Keep your lower back soft, to move with the horse, but your shoulders straight."

After a little practice, Dan decided that the rhythm of posting was not unlike the rhythm of sex. Forward, back, forward, back.

"Heels down! And your legs are swinging," Dorothy called.

Except that during sex nobody critiqued his posture or his form. His partner generally vocalized things along the lines of, "Oh, yes!" instead of snorting and drooling green foam. Of course, he generally didn't have his women harnessed, with a bit in the mouth, either.

Miz Lilia sat in the small bleachers outside the ring, glancing up occasionally from her laptop to check on his progress.

He felt like a damned fool in the boots and the helmet, wiggling his butt around for all to see. *The bloody English strike again.* He should show up in London with a chaw of tobacco in his mouth and his Western saddle. He'd teach the pasty-faced snots how to ride like real men. *Maybe I'll rope and tie Lovely Nigel and toss him in a pile of manure. I'd really enjoy that.*

They warmed up the horse—and him—for a few more minutes and then Dorothy directed him over the two jumps that she'd called an "in-and-out."

"Lean forward," she called. "Hands higher on his neck, heels down!"

Tricks sailed over it, Dan flying with him. It was real fun, until he lost his balance slightly and popped himself in the balls on the forward edge of the saddle.

"Gyaaahooow!" Dan reflexively pulled back on the reins. Tricks didn't know quite what to make of the sound or the signal, so he stopped dead, right before the second jump. Dan, now clutching his balls with one hand and holding the reins in the other, sailed right over his neck, bounced off the rail of the jump and landed ignominiously in the sand of the ring.

Tricks backed up a step, twitched his sizable nostrils and then snorted smelly green spit-foam onto his rider.

Dan scrambled up and shot a glance toward Lil to see if she'd noticed. Great. She was running toward him, laptop left on the bleachers.

"Are you all right?"

Dorothy ran over, too.

Dan wiped the green horse-spit off his shoulder and chest and wished he could wipe the red off his face, too. "I'm fine," he growled. "I haven't lost my seat on a horse since I was—"

"Fifteen years old." Lil nodded.

"You popped him in the mouth," said Dorothy, shaking her head.

"Yeah, well, the saddle caught me in the— Never mind." Furious with himself and embarrassed as hell, he could barely speak.

Even the damn horse seemed to look at him sideways, the equine message loud and clear. *And you call yourself a horseman?*

He stalked over to Tricks and swung himself right back into the saddle. He couldn't believe how many times he'd now made an ass out of himself in front of

Lilia London. Bad enough that he sucked at her refinement lessons. But did he have to look incompetent on a horse, too?

Stiff with embarrassment, he said to Dorothy, "Okay, let's take it again."

He circled the ring at a slow canter and then urged Tricks toward the jumps for the second time. As they took the first one, a loud, disgusting, rumbling noise came from behind him and the horse swished his tail. Dan's grouchiness faded into amusement at the look on Lilia's face: Tricks backfired yet again over the second oxer and Dan almost collapsed laughing on the animal's neck—which didn't help his form any.

"Sit up," Dorothy called. "Shoulders back! Heels down!"

"Yeah, yeah," Dan said. "You may have a fainter on your hands, there. Miss Manners has never seen a horse fart."

Two bright spots of color appeared at Lil's cheekbones. "I'm nowhere close to fainting, thank you very much! Oh, *eeeeuuuuuuwwwww!*"

Dan heard solid little plops behind him in the ring and grinned. "How do you like them apples?" he called.

Lil packed up her laptop and retreated to the stable's air-conditioned office, where she didn't have to see or smell such things.

"Priss-pot," Dan muttered under his breath. "Can't handle a little horse poop. Can't sit on a man's face. What exactly am I doing with this woman? Oh, yeah. Making an ass out of myself. How could I have forgotten?"

Dorothy directed him to take a higher jump, setting wooden rails into position on a frame.

He started Tricks toward it.

"Come in faster for this one—it's bigger and you'll need the momentum."

Dan squeezed the horse's sides with his legs and they picked up speed. He began to lean forward as they approached, putting all his weight into his heels in the stirrups.

"Good," Dorothy called.

Tricks lived up to his name and veered to the right at the last possible moment, almost unseating Dan. This time, though, he moved with the horse, swung him around sharply and took him right back to the fence. They were up and then airborne, coming down in perfect form on the other side.

"Great work, Dan!"

He nodded his thanks, automatically looking around for Lil to see if she'd actually witnessed him do something competent outside of the bedroom. But no—that's right. She'd gone to the office. It was Murphy's Law.

She'd continue to think of him as a well-endowed moron with only one talent and no style. Dan sighed. *I might as well go on and get that pouch of Red Man, wad a big ol' chaw in my cheek and really impress her. I'll spit in one of her fancy-ass china tea cups. She won't mind a bit.*

He finished his English riding lesson with a lot more aplomb than when he'd started, but it didn't matter since she wasn't around to see.

13

SHANNON'S REVENGE was not pretty. It sat on Lil's desk, Day-Glo orange with…dear God…several attachments. They all radiated from a bouquet of fake plastic daisies in a Windex-blue vase.

Unfortunately there was no doubt whatsoever as to what the object was, although Lil had never actually seen one before. She clutched at her throat and the blood drained from her face as she came nose to nose with a vibrator for the first time in her life.

She shrank back, aghast, at the attachment with bumps, the one with a curved tip, and the one with—ugh! ugh! ugh!—two protrusions for simultaneous penetration of two different orifices.

Lil didn't even want to touch them! Did women really… No, surely not? It was depraved, indecent, horrifying! Oooh, but what was that particular attachment there? It had a wider head, and might feel good on a girl's—

Lilia Lisbeth London! Are you possessed by a sexual Satan? How can you even think such things? Did she need to have an exorcism?

"Shannon!" She didn't yell, as a lady never raised her

voice, but she infused it with enough annoyance and acid that she felt sure the point got across. "Did rice cakes really deserve *this?*"

Shan poked her head around Lil's doorway and grinned lasciviously. "One hundred percent. I had skipped not one but *two* meals when I spied that Krispy Kreme box. I was desperate for fat, sugar, sustenance in general. And then to open it up and find cardboard! I almost cried. Ask Jane."

Lil pointed without speaking at the awful device on her desk. "That's…obscene. Vile. Gross!"

"Oh, bullshit. You need one, Lil. Every modern woman has one."

"I'm not touching it. Please remove it from my desk and take it away. Joke's over."

Down the hall, they heard the front door open.

"That better be Jane!"

Shannon turned and looked.

"Haaaaaaaaa," came Dan's voice.

Lil paled and stared at the vibrator bouquet. "Shit!"

Shannon's head popped back in. "Did you just say—"

"Shit! Yes!" Lil peeled off her suit jacket in record time and flung it over the bouquet. She couldn't possibly let Dan Granger see that. She would simply die if he did.

Not that it would shock him—his request of yesterday was far more shocking—but he would probably try to suggest a play date with the items! And that was one thing she simply could not handle.

"Haaaaaaaa," Shan mimicked. "How yew doin' thar, Dan?"

Lilia clapped a hand to her forehead. "Has it ever occurred to you that it's bad for business to insult clients?"·

"Oh, just peachy, thunk you, Miss Shane. And you?" Dan said it in a flawless, stuffy Long Island Lock-Jaw.

Lil burst out laughing, and Shan did, too.

"I should like my wardrobe returned, you evil vixen," he added, still in Lock-Jaw.

Shannon smiled serenely. "I feel your pain, Dan. But no. I've put together a much better wardrobe for you. You'll love it." She turned to Lil. "Everything's in my office. I've got to go to an appointment, so help yourself. Oh—" she winked "—and don't forget your jacket when you leave the office. It's a little cool out this morning."

Lil looked daggers at her. "Thank you, hon."

"No problem. Ta ta!"

"Mornin,' Lil," said Dan.

"Good morning," she said with a gracious smile. "Would you like some coffee?"

"Yes, please. Though I'da rather have had it in bed with you."

Her smile vanished. "Cream or sugar?" she asked woodenly. She had to end the physical part of their relationship. That was clear.

"Just hot 'n' black, darlin'. Say, isn't it bad manners not to remember how someone takes their coffee after you've been extremely, uh, intimate with him?"

"Yes, but it's worse manners to point that out," said Lil, coloring but standing her ground. She changed the subject. "So are you suffering any ill-effects from your fall?"

"Just a bruised shoulder and a terminal case of shame."

"You don't have to be embarrassed."

Dan grunted. "So what's on tap for today?"

"We have another English riding lesson for you, another dance lesson and we've got to try all of those clothes on you that Shannon purchased. We'll also have lunch and dinner at elegant restaurants so that you're able to practice your table manners some more."

"You're not gonna make me eat any more of those hairy salad weeds, are you?"

Lil shook her head. "No, but you have to promise not to grunt like a caveman."

"When—"

"Just now. When I told you that you needn't be embarrassed about the fall."

"Like a *caveman?*"

Her lips twitched. "Perhaps the sound was more warthog than actual man."

"Hey, now, Miss Manners! You're fallin' off your own high horse. That ain't so polite."

She shot him a rueful glance. "Oh, dear, you're right. My apologies…" She wasn't doing well this morning, was she? She'd cursed and she was now behaving like Shannon. She sighed.

"And maybe we should talk about the animal sounds that *you* make, say, in bed."

Heat swept over her face and she was bereft of speech.

"I won't go so far as to say warthog, but there's definitely some kitten in there, and some—"

"Mr. Granger, let's please drop this subject immediately!"

He grinned. Then he cocked an eyebrow at her. "We're back to Mr. Granger, are we? That's not what you called me the other night, Lil."

She put her hands up to her incinerated cheeks and ran to shut her office door. She took a deep breath before she turned to face him again. "We need to put that night behind us, Dan. I can't function in a business relationship with you while also…ah…being intimate. It just doesn't work for me. I hope you can understand."

His jaw tightened and his lips flattened. "Sure. Even we unsophisticated country boys can comprehend when we're gettin' the brush-off. I do apologize for shockin' your delicate, uh, sensibilities with my terrible request that you sit—"

"Dan!"

He stopped. "But I was only trying to give you pleasure. And as a guy who's often up to the elbows inside a cow, trying to deliver her calf, it just doesn't seem that outrageous to me."

Up to the elbows in a cow's—ugh! Lil swallowed.

"It's part of life," he added.

Not part of my life. "Thank you, Dan. I—I appreciate that." *But it also illustrates why we should just cut this sexual liaison off right now, before it gets any messier. Because we have nothing, absolutely nothing in common.*

"You *appreciate* that?" He blinked at her. Then his expression got even darker.

Too late, she realized that her attempt to be polite had delivered a rude slap to him.

"No, Lilia. You appreciate a man holding the door open for you. You appreciate a word of thanks. But you don't goddamn *appreciate* a man's desire to give you oral sex." He expelled a short, unamused bark of laughter. "It just ain't the right word, darlin'."

"Dan, I'm sorry. I didn't mean—"

"Even to a country boy, that sounds patronizing and dismissive. So you can just keep your appreciation to yourself." He got up and headed for her door.

"Dan, please! Where are you going?"

"To get my cup of hot, black coffee, Miz London. Do I have your royal permission?"

"I'll get it," she said, moving from behind her desk to put a hand on his arm. The moment she touched him, even through his shirtsleeve, she knew it had been a mistake.

He stared into her eyes, breathing heavily in his anger. She stared into his, with regret and hot awareness. What she wanted to do was kiss him and run her hands over his naked, furred chest. Feel all of him inside her again.

He broke the eye contact first and shifted away from her touch. "I don't want you to wait on me. I'll get the coffee myself—unless you're afraid I'll break some more of your dishes." Dan opened the door and headed down the hallway to the kitchenette.

There was nothing to do but follow him. They each got their coffee in silence and then she suggested that he try on all the clothes in Shannon's office before they headed over to see Jean Pierre.

Dan shrugged. "Fine. But I hope she's got a suit of armor in there so the French fruitcake can't touch me."

"Maybe you should take his interest in you as a compliment."

"Huh."

Lil gave up on that angle and walked to the small rolling rack in Shan's office, where her partner had hung Dan's new clothes. She fingered a beautiful charcoal cashmere sweater, some shirts that were works of art in terms of fabric and tailoring, and three pairs of casual slacks that looked as if they'd each cost more than her monthly car payment.

Shan had also bought him silk T-shirts, a couple of casual but expensive blazers, gorgeous leather belts and shoes.

Dan made the mistake of looking at a couple of price tags during the process and almost passed out in shock. "There's a down payment on a piece of real estate, here!"

"Not quite," Lil said, passing him a shirt to try on. To her chagrin, Dan whipped off the one he was wearing before she could leave the room, and she was faced with that quite edible chest again. The saliva in her mouth evaporated and refused to return, even with repeated swallowing.

Dan raised a brow at her. "What? Surely you don't expect me to dress in the powder room when you've already seen every part of me?"

"Shh. But Jane's right down the hall! And we just discussed returning to an all-business relationship."

"No, you discussed it. I just listened." And Dan put on the new shirt, unavoidably flexing all that delicious chest and shoulder muscle at her. "Give me the first pair of pants, please, Lil."

She thrust them at him and turned around before he dropped the ones he was wearing. She just didn't need to see him in his boxers right now, especially since they had that convenient little peephole that often revealed a man's goods.

When she turned back around, he smirked at her. She pursed her lips.

Bit by bit, Dan assumed a mantle of style and elegance that he wore surprisingly well. Shannon had done him proud, and everything fit him superbly with the exception of one pair of shoes.

Dan flexed his feet in them and grimaced. "These are downright painful. They're not wide enough." He sat down in Shannon's yellow leather office chair and pulled them off, beautiful Italian lace-ups in a rich chestnut-brown leather.

Lil found herself riveted by his strong, broad hands—still scarred in spite of the small repairs the manicure had made—and his powerful thighs.

Her very uncooperative brain refused all her efforts to repress the memory of how she'd sat spread-eagled on his knees in the Mustang. And how he'd felt, sliding into her inch by inch.

Dan sat up after replacing the shoes in their box. He quirked an eyebrow. "Penny for your thoughts, Lil."

Oh, no. You couldn't even give me a hundred dollars for these thoughts. Because they're starting to get X-rated. "Oh, I was just thinking of some errands I have to run in the next couple of days. Dry cleaners, post office, you know."

"Yeah. I always look lustful when I think about the post office, too."

"I beg your pardon?"

"No need. I happen to find being coveted by a beautiful woman very stimulating."

Lil crossed her arms over her chest. "I do not covet you, Mr. Granger."

"Oh? Well, I'm afraid the rest of me is attached to that one part that you were, uh, drinking in. It doesn't snap on and off."

"I don't covet that, either! And you're utterly impossible." Lil glared at him, tucked her hair behind her ears and looked at her watch. "We've got to leave for the stables, now."

"Oh, joy."

She exited Shannon's office and went into her own to get her pocketbook and keys. Shannon's dirty bouquet still sat on her desk, hidden by her suit jacket.

Dan followed her in, patting various pockets. "Did I leave my shades in here?"

"I haven't seen—"

"Oh, there they are, on your desk."

Lil wanted to get out of there as fast as possible, so she moved to the door. Despite her rapid exit strategy, Dan said the words she least wanted to hear.

"Here, don't forget your blazer."

She closed her eyes and winced, her back to him.

"My, my, my," said Granger, his voice strangled with amusement. "What do we have here?"

14

"I CAN EXPLAIN that," said Lil, who wished that the floor would open up and swallow her for brunch. She didn't even care if it burped afterward.

"You *can?*" Dan's voice exuded fascination. "Oh, I can't wait to hear this."

Lil stared at the Day-Glo orange monstrosity and its happy attachments and wished a certain blonde a gruesome death. Perhaps clad in shiny pink polyester and blue gingham accessories. And definitely in cheap, nasty shoes. Flat ones.

I hate you, Shannon. Lil closed her eyes and tried to relieve her feelings by adding a lousy haircut, a bad dye job and oversize, suntan-colored panty hose to Shan's burial outfit.

"Would you believe that a marketing company selected my name randomly as a single woman and asked me to test the product?"

Dan considered it and then shook his head. "No."

"How about believing that it isn't mine?"

"Nope. It belongs to you, or you wouldn't be the color of a West Texas sunset."

Lil cleared her throat. "Okay. Then would you believe that Shannon put it on my desk as payback for the rice cakes I left in the Krispy Kreme box?"

He rubbed at his chin. "Maybe. That woman is evil."

"Yes, she is. And I need your help to come up with something worse than this in order to pay her back."

"Done," he said. "I still owe her for giving away my suitcases. But in the meantime, would you have any interest in, uh, trying out Big O there with company?"

"No!"

He sighed. "You're no fun."

"Just because I'm not perverted doesn't mean I'm no fun!"

Dan stared at her and laughed. "Lil, playing with your boyfriend and a couple of toys isn't perverted. It's pretty harmless, in fact."

"You're not my boyfriend!"

His face shuttered. "Right."

"You're my client."

"Uh-huh."

"And…and we're late. We have to go."

"After you, your highness."

"Don't call me that, please."

"My apologies, milady."

Lil badly wanted to stomp her foot, but she controlled herself. Ladies did not stamp their feet, nor did they scream, nor did they kill their clients or business partners even when sorely tempted.

They got into the Mustang and headed out toward the stables. Dan looked pensive as they drove, a half smile on his face. As they turned into the gates of Central

Pines Stables and progressed down the white-fenced driveway he tried one more time.

"That, um, bumpy attachment sure looked like fun. You sure you don't want to get together and—"

"I'm quite sure. Now stop it, Dan. This is starting to feel like harassment."

"Sorry, darlin'. We professors emeritus of Uncivilization 101 can get too enthusiastic over our subject matter at times."

Lil made no comment as he parked the car next to the large concrete pad with rails where the horses were bathed. A huge dun that Dan said was a Holsteiner cross gelding was tethered there while a stable hand rinsed soap off his massive back.

His eyes were sleepy and the only movement he made now and then was a casual lip-twitch or a swat with his tail.

They got out of the car as the stable hand ambled off for something.

"You gonna disappear into the office again, afraid of a little equine odor?"

"No. I like animals. I've just never been exposed to…" Lil searched for a proper word. "To…"

"Horseshit?"

"Dan! Language."

"Yes, I used some." He grinned unrepentantly and chucked her under the chin.

She wasn't used to chin-chucking, either. "I'd never been exposed to horse by-products before, so I'm afraid that I found it disgusting."

Dan looked just beyond her, at the big dun animal, and hooted with laughter.

She turned. "What's so funny?"

"Big Boy, there—well, he likes you. And he's very relaxed."

It took Lil a moment to register that the equine was dangling its quite enormous reproductive organ in the most complacent, unashamed way!

She couldn't help staring at the monstrous penis.

Dan hooted again and she closed her eyes. "That is…that is *repellent!*"

"Catherine the Great didn't think so. You are so damned cute when you're shocked, Lil."

"Where did it come from? He didn't have that a moment ago—I would have noticed it when we drove in!"

"Horses have a sheath, Lil. He just happens to have dropped his Mr. Happy down because he's feeling relaxed."

"I thought you said he was a gelding!"

"He is. But that just means they cut off the poor bastard's balls, not his tool."

"Well, can't you persuade him to retract it again?"

Dan got a good laugh out of that.

"I'm so glad to be a source of amusement for you," she said in acid tones.

"Chill, Lil."

Dorothy spied them from the barn and came over to join them and show Dan where his assigned horse was.

"Tricks again?" he asked.

"No. This time you'll be on Sonata. She's a sweetheart, very smooth gaits. She's the chestnut in stall number eighteen. You know where the tack room is?"

Dad nodded.

"Okay, then. I'll see you in the ring in just a few minutes."

Lil dusted off a spot on the bleachers and prepared to watch the lesson. Dan took off his cowboy boots and slid his feet into the polished black English riding boots, which looked wrong on him in so many ways. He still refused to wear the breeches, and she was oddly, secretly relieved. She didn't know if she'd laugh or cry to see him in full chase regalia. Again, she wondered why Dan cared about impressing his mother, father and sister. He was so irrepressibly Texas alpha male that it just didn't fit his character.

And he had such a chip on his shoulder about the English that it would be borderline comical—if the chip weren't rooted in a soul-deep pain. He'd been a kid abandoned by his mother, who'd taken off for greener English pastures. Was he here with Lil to prove that his mother had made a mistake? That he was every bit as good as this man Nigel, her husband?

Lil was afraid so. And that realization made her heart twist and turn over. Under all that cocky Western bravado and sexual aggression beat the heart of a boy who'd been rejected, found wanting.

Despite the incongruity of the English riding boots on Dan, and the smaller European saddle, even Lil could tell that he was a damn good rider. Yesterday's fall had been an aberration. For today, once he got his heels down and his hands into position, he moved as one with the horse. At a canter, which was what Dorothy called the gait midway between a trot and a gallop, Dan's seat didn't come out of the saddle an inch and his lower back seemed fluid, supple, absorbing all the shock of Sonata's hooves hitting the ground.

Sitting on the bleachers and watching him ride, Lil began to get aroused despite her best efforts not to. His long legs astride the horse, the power of his hands, the way the bulge at his groin sat the saddle.

What was wrong with her? And why did she picture him astride *her,* in her soft bed at home?

She truly had to get beyond this. She'd walked a few steps on the wild side, at least her pretty tame version of it. She'd finally had some incredible sex. So she needed to move on. Because getting attached to some cowpoke who lived on a Texas ranch was just…silly. Immature.

She was a modern woman, not the heroine of a fairy-tale romance. A pity, but there were realities to be faced, and her happily-ever-after did not include this cowboy client with the magic mouth and hands.

She watched Dan take several fences on Sonata, murmuring to her and patting her for a job well done. He'd even brought a couple of apples for her, which still resided on the dashboard of the Mustang. He was a good man. He was an incredibly sexy man. He just couldn't be *her* man. After all, he was leaving for his sister's wedding at the end of a week. And then she'd never see him again.

Would you have any interest in trying out Big O with company?

Not really. Because it would be such a poor, plastic substitute for you.

She shamelessly ogled his butt as he posted past her side of the ring, and felt heat bloom between her thighs. *Great, Lil. You're jealous of a horse, now? Oh, Nana would be so proud.*

Nana would never know. Lil massaged her temples. And thank God for that. She did miss her so very much…but there was an utterly awful kernel of relief within her, relief at finally, after so many years of being the model granddaughter and not wanting to cause Nana any trouble— Oh, God. Could she even *think* this without being struck down by lightning?

Lil gulped. She tried to shove away that horrible tremor of relief that she now finally had the freedom to be her own person. To not have to express gratitude and obedience every day to the woman who had raised her since she'd been a colicky infant.

No matter how sweet and loving Nana Lisbeth had been, she'd never let Lil forget that she'd been an unexpected burden to an old woman. That Lil owed her pretty behavior and respect. Nana, in her gentle way, had been an exacting task-mistress and a benign dictator.

DAN LOUNGED on his hotel bed, watching ESPN and trying not to think about Lilia and the hot-orange vibrator. He wasn't under any illusion that she'd touch it, much less use it, but a man could sure fantasize.

A man could also get blue balls by doing that, and he was damned if he'd jack off like some horny teenager. However, he had an irritating, persistent erection and he needed to make it go away before it deranged him.

What was the best way to deflate a real bastard of a hard-on? Dan sighed. He reached for his cell phone and called his mother.

Sure enough, before he'd even gotten past the country code, his fat lead pipe had wilted into overcooked linguine.

"Hallooo?" she answered herself on the third ring.

Great Scot—wherever were the servants when ya needed 'em? "Haaa, Mama. How you doin'?"

"Daniel! What a lovely surprise."

I'll bet. Did I catch you painting your nails? Oh, no— your manicurist would do that for you. Dan quickly bypassed the sordid memory that he'd had a manicure recently, too. He cleared his throat. "Uh, yeah. Listen, I was wondering what to get Claire for a weddin' gift."

"She's registered at Harrod's, darling. Get her, oh, I don't know—the silver punch bowl, perhaps?"

"Does anybody still use those things?"

"Yes, of course, Daniel. In finer homes."

Homes unlike the one I live in, eh? "Well, all right, then. I'll do that."

"Are you working with Miss London, Daniel?"

Not, are you happy? Are you healthy? What's new in your life? But "are you going to embarrass us?" "Yes, I am, Mama. And she's doing wonders with even such raw, rude material as me."

"There's no need for your sarcasm, Daniel."

"How's Claire?" he asked, changing the subject. "She gettin' any preweddin' jitters?"

"Claire is fine. Are you going to work on your accent?"

His blood started to simmer. "Mama, I was born in West Texas, same as you. And I don't know how much time it took you to speak like the queen, but I'll bet it was more than two weeks."

A long pause ensued. "Well, it's of no consequence. You just take after your father's side of the family."

Dan's blood came to a full boil and he gritted his teeth, clenching the tiny phone so hard that if it had been alive, it surely would have squeaked. "Is that what you're gonna tell people? That my unfortunate speech patterns come from Dad, who was just a passing weakness in your life? The trailer trash you left behind? That's beautiful, Mama."

"Daniel, I don't like the tone you're taking with me. Now, I've got to toddle on, my dear. I'll tell Claire you sent your love. *Ciao.*"

And just like that, the line went dead. Dan resisted the urge to stomp on his cell phone and smash it into a couple hundred little pieces.

"The friggin' rain in friggin' Spain fell gently on the friggin' plains." Dan got off the bed and headed for the shower, his third that day after the stables and then the dancing lesson with the French-fried Fruitcake.

Jolly friggin' good, then. He was going to another up-tight white tablecloth place with Miz Lilia. Maybe he'd toss the dinner rolls at unsuspecting patrons, and suck the wine right out of the bottle. Maybe he'd tie his napkin around his neck like a handkerchief on a dog.

Muttering, Dan stripped off his clothes and got into the shower. There was no way he was gonna remember all Lil's BS rules. What he needed was for her to come with him and keep him out of trouble.

He froze, the soap clamped under his left armpit. Of course. According to the fussy formal invite, he was welcome to bring a date to this blasted wedding. Who better to bring than Lilia London? Now, all he had to do was convince her that she wanted to take a short holiday to Britain.

15

DAN MADE SURE to be on his very best behavior that evening. He did not bring up the orange dildo. He did not tease Lil about anything. He told her how beautiful she looked.

He carefully placed his napkin on his lap, ordered from the wine list with aplomb and even ate the nasty peppery weed things in his salad without complaining.

He did not drink from the bottle or throw the dinner rolls. He even tried to speak more like Lilia and less like himself.

At last cappuccino and dessert arrived. He stirred the weird little crystallized sugar stick around in the coffee and pretended that he wasn't impatient as hell for the damn thing to go ahead and melt before next year. He lifted the cup with his pinky curved out, and watched her watch him with silent approval—but also puzzlement.

Finally she asked, "Dan, you're doing such a lovely job tonight that I have to wonder one of two things. First, are you feeling all right? And second, is there something you want from me…besides sex?"

Well, there goes my smooth segue. Damn it.

Dan eyed the slice of chocolate torte in front of him

for a moment before meeting her gaze. It tapered into a point as sharp as her question. The thin wafer on top of it was as dark as her eyes. He found her more tempting.

Step carefully and don't make a hash out of this, man.

He quirked his mouth and leaned back slightly in his chair. "As a matter of fact, I have a proposal for you."

Her eyes radiated wariness.

"A decent one." He smiled.

She didn't.

"You've taught me a lot, Lil. You have given this diamond-in-the-rough a lot of polish. But there's only so much you can do with a cowboy in a couple of weeks. I can dress better and stop saying 'ain't,' but I'm still no Cary Grant. And my mo—uh, my family—they tend to get my goat without half-trying. Which can be socially dangerous. So I'm wondering if you'd like to take an all-expenses-paid trip to England…as my date for the wedding."

She opened her mouth, but he held up a hand. "I promise you that if you come, I'll be a perfect gentleman. You can have your own hotel room, no strings attached. Believe it or not, I am capable of taking 'no' for an answer. Even if I don't like it."

She put down her fork, lifted her cappuccino cup to her lips and eyed him over the rim. "I don't know, Dan."

"I'll make it worth your while. I'll pay you. We'll fly first-class. Shoot, I'll even throw in some shopping on Bond Street and a Big Ben shot glass." He grinned.

"Dan, you know I could never go shopping on your tab. That's out of the question."

"Why?"

"Because I'm not your wife or your daughter!"

"So?"

"Dan. It would be…behaving like your mistress. There's an element of sleaziness to it. Do you see?"

"No. It's a gift."

"It's not a gift. A gift is something you choose, wrap and present for a special occasion."

"But I'd screw that up, I know it. Better for you to choose."

"Maybe I'm just hopelessly old-fashioned, but I can't accept a shopping spree from you."

"Unless I marry you first."

Her eyes flew to his, startled, and he laughed. "You're just so damned cute with all your strange little rules. Most women would jump at the chance to grab my credit cards for the afternoon."

She sipped her cappuccino. "I do thank you for the offer. It's very kind of you."

He sighed. "But socially unacceptable. See, that's what I'm talking about. I had no idea! That's why I need you to come with me to the wedding. You can stomp on my toe or jab me in the butt with your pocketbook when I screw up."

Lil came close to spitting her coffee onto her dessert, but she managed to swallow it, her shoulders shaking. "Dan, you're doing very well, really. And I could never do physical violence to you in the name of etiquette—"

"It sorta defeats the purpose, don't it?"

"In a word, yes. There are more subtle signals."

"Lilia, you know by now that I can't even spell the word subtle."

Her eyes twinkled.

"So you'll come?"

She sighed. "Dan, I've already put off my vacation once. And given the, um, physical tension between us, my traveling to England with you is simply not a good idea."

"But I need you. And I'll pay for that vacation of yours later. And I promise to be a gentleman."

"Mmm." She toyed with her own slice of chocolate torte, taking a bit onto her fork but then laying it down on the dessert plate again. He knew she wanted it—he'd learned by now that she loved chocolate—so why wouldn't she allow herself the pleasure? She wasn't in any danger at all of getting fat.

"The problem inherent in your request, Dan, and indeed, in our working relationship, is that…oh, dear. Should I really say this? You've hired me to transform you into a gentleman. But I like you so much more as a rude, sexually-charged, tasty cowboy."

Lilia took her napkin and put it casually, correctly to the left of her plate while he stared at her.

Seeming surprised at her own words, she reached for her tiny handbag, her elegant, shiny hair swinging as she bent to retrieve it. "Will you excuse me while I find the ladies' room?"

And he gazed after her as the confounded woman walked away from the table, her rear view something to be framed for *Vogue* or *Harper's Bazaar. Tasty?*

LIL WALKED like a lady all the way to the ladies' room, but once inside she collapsed on the velvet fainting couch, since she felt like, well, fainting.

Had she really just said that to Dan Granger? But it was true. There was something about the man that held enormous appeal for her. He was larger than life, crude, rude and…unbelievably sweet. Sexy as *hell*. She might not be able to *do* it, but it made her hot and breathless that he'd asked her to sit on his beautifully shaped, reckless, hedonistic mouth.

Lil squirmed and pressed her thighs together, just as the door opened and another woman came in.

She glanced at Lil and enquired, "Are you all right?"

Lil nodded. "Yes, thank you for asking." *I just have a terminal case of cowboy. It's most improper, and being proper just happens to be my job.*

She pulled a compact and some lipstick from her bag while the woman went on to one of the stalls. She stared at her tiny, circular reflection and the features that had always marked her as different from the Anglo-Saxon girls at school, kept a lot of the Anglo-Saxon boys from asking her out. She had tiny, precise lips, almond-shaped eyes, blue-black hair. She looked like her mother, with her father's more Anglo nose.

There was nothing so remarkable about her face that Dan Granger should think it wildly beautiful. And nothing about her thin, virtually hairless body that should make him crave her. It was far easier for her to pinpoint what it was about *him* that drew her.

For if one were to burn the dreadful belt with his name on it, he could appear as a particularly tanned Olympian on a white, marble, Greek pediment…though he'd be the only one wearing ropers and a big, dashing hat.

Lil blinked and realized that by now, she'd put on an awful lot of lipstick. In fact, she looked like a small, half-Vietnamese Bozo. She reached for a tissue and wiped it off.

She'd really gotten herself into a pickle, now. Because she'd told Dan straight out that she liked him in the raw, so to speak. But her job was to turn him into filet mignon with a stylish garnish.

And she'd also basically admitted to him that she liked his sexual pursuit of her, embarrassing as it was at times. So if she were to go on this trip to England, things were bound to be…complicated.

Mortifying, but it had taken someone with his unbelievable brashness to get through her nice-girl defenses. And get through them he had.

Lil washed her hands, straightened her skirt and smoothed her hair, having come to no useful conclusions at all. Bottom line: she shouldn't have said what she'd said to him. What was wrong with her?

It was as if some long-buried, renegade voice was bubbling up inside of her and making itself heard at the least opportune moments. It was most unwelcome…and worse, the voice wasn't always polite.

She made her way back to the table, where Dan sat fielding glances from women all over the restaurant. The sixty-year-old in the back corner with the diamonds, the woman in her mid-forties with the cleavage and even a woman in her twenties who was there with a good-looking date.

While she was partly proud, an unfamiliar territorial feeling swept through Lil. She wanted to taser each of the women, sending the sixty-year-old nosefirst into her lamb entrée, Ms. Cleavage into her salad and the cute young thing into her grilled portobello.

Lil pasted a serene, genteel smile on her face to disguise her malicious thoughts. Dan got up and pulled out her chair for her—very nice. She sat down at the table and he eased the chair in a couple of inches as she'd taught him.

"Would you like a cognac?" he asked.

"That would be lovely, thank you."

Dan signaled the waiter just by raising a brow. "Yes, the lady would like a cognac, Courvoisier VSOP, please."

"And for you, sir?"

"No, thank you. The lady herself goes to my head."

Oh, my. Her lips twitched. "Aren't you smooth tonight?"

He simply smiled at her. The Dan she was used to would have turned her words against her and into some sexual invitation. Where was he? He'd turned his inner wolf into a lapdog.

Lil realized suddenly that he was still on his best behavior so that she'd agree to go to the wedding with him. How could she explain to him that while she hadn't approved of his raunchy pursuit of her, she'd liked it because it made her feel desired for the first time in her life?

Her cognac arrived and she took a sip of it. Wait, what was she thinking? She wasn't about to explain *anything* to Dan, except for why she was most certainly *not* accompanying him to England. Because she didn't do casual sex, there was no future in this relationship, and he stole from her the very thing she needed to make her living: her status and identity as a lady.

"So." Dan interrupted her musings. "I just want to say that I'm flattered—no, touched—that you like me the way that I am. But you don't *approve* of me the way I am, do you, Lil?"

She opened her mouth and closed it again. How was she supposed to answer that, for Heaven's sake?

"Approval is a whole different ball game, isn't it? And approval connotes respect. Well, I want your respect, Lil, about as bad as I want…other things. So I'm asking you to keep working with me. To come to England not only as my date, as my guest, but as my coach."

Still she said nothing. She picked up her fork again and pushed at the chocolate torte. It looked delicious. But it was empty calories, and she'd had doughnuts this week.

"Would you just go ahead and *eat* some of that? It's not a capital offense, for crying out loud."

Her eyes flew to his, which were half amused, half annoyed. "I—"

"You deny yourself pleasure. Why?"

"I do not. I slept with you. I just ate a wonderful meal and I'm sipping cognac."

"Let me rephrase that. You skimp on pleasure. You

tantalize yourself with it, and then you put it just out of reach, like you don't deserve it or something. What is up with that?"

"I don't know what you're talking about."

"Okay, whatever you say. But eat your damn cake. It's delicious and you'll insult me if you let it go to waste. You'll insult the chef, too."

Lil had forgotten to put her napkin back in her lap. She did so and looked again at the slice of cake, which winked at her like a wedge of sin. She *didn't* want to insult anyone. She put a bite of it into her mouth and the rich flavor seduced her immediately.

"Atta girl." He grinned.

She could feel the cake landing with an evil splat right on her hips, but told herself that men didn't like swizzle-stick women whose ribs and elbows poked them in bed. Right?

"Now, back to the topic of England. When was the last time you left the country, Lil?"

"High school," she admitted. She'd gone with a study-abroad class to Paris, but they'd been heavily organized, scheduled and chaperoned. Since then she'd been afraid to go too far because of Nana Lisbeth's age and health.

"High school. So it's been years. I tell you what. You come with me to England, and we'll have a good time. A good platonic time. Then I'll send you on a trip for a couple of weeks to anywhere you want to go. What do you want to see most in the world, Lil?"

"Vietnam," she said. "My mother's birthplace. I've

been brought up utterly American—the other side of my heritage has always been…swept under the rug. My grandmother never, ever said so, but I think she was shocked when her son married outside of his culture, outside of his country. I have relatives in Vietnam who I've never even met. I don't speak the language. I regret that."

She ate another bite of chocolate cake. And another. "I think that's why I'm so interested in the customs and etiquette of other countries. I have always felt somewhat *other*. Outside of the mainstream. Not white, like all the kids I went to school with. Not white like my grandmother."

"Who cares what color you are? You're beautiful." Dan reached across the table and took her free hand, looking like the embodiment of all her youthful, girlish dreams.

Her pulse kicked up, and she ate more of the chocolate torte so she wouldn't eat him. So he was rude, crude and socially unacceptable. So what? She was acceptable, even desired, by him.

"I'll be forever in your debt if you come to England with me, Lil. Let's explore another culture together. Then you go on your own personal journey to find your roots. All expenses paid. No strings attached."

She put down her fork, all the cake gone, and hesitated. She pulled her hand gently from his, and his face fell, the glow in his eyes dimming.

"Okay, Dan. I'll go to England with you."

Dan blinked in surprise, then let out a whoop that had every head in the elegant dining room turning their way. Lil resisted the urge to crawl under the table.

He cleared his throat. "Sorry. I'm just excited. And elated. Thank you."

She couldn't help but smile at the man, even though she wasn't at all sure what she'd just gotten herself into.

He smiled back. Then he reached a hand across the table and used his index finger to wipe something from the corner of her mouth. "You got chocolate on your face, Lil. I think it's real cute."

He popped the finger into his mouth. "Tastes good, too. We could always ask the chef for a bucket of icing, stop to get a paintbrush on the way back to the hotel, and have a lot of fun together naked." He waggled his brows.

Dan's inner wolf had gobbled the lapdog in a single bite. He was back in rare form…but she couldn't tell him that she was relieved.

"No, Dan," Lil said.

He shrugged as if to say it had been worth the try, and nodded to their waiter. "Check, please."

16

LIL'S EYES WIDENED as she and Dan entered the Terraces Lounge, British Airways' luxury waiting area for first-class travelers. As far as she knew, they were in JFK Airport, but the Terraces transported them to another planet.

A cross between a bar and a full-service spa, the lounge featured reclining lounge chairs under white umbrellas, trickling water fountains and the scent of freshly cut grass. She even heard birds chirping, though it seemed unlikely that they were nestling behind the übermodern steel bar among the pricey liquor bottles.

"Sweet, ain't it?" said Dan. "I mean, *isn't* it."

Sweet, indeed. And exclusive.

"Would you like a preflight massage?" he asked.

"Excuse me?"

"They have reflexology, too."

Lil wasn't sure she wanted some unknown person manhandling her body or her feet. "No, thank you."

"There you go, denying yourself pleasure again. How about a drink? You seemed to like that cognac a few nights ago."

Yes, but it had made her so drunk that she'd almost

lost all resolve and ordered that bucket of chocolate icing from the chef.

"A cognac for the lady, please." Dan was already ordering. "And a margarita for me. Top shelf, with salt."

She wasn't sure why, but she wanted to drink what he was drinking. Share something with him. "Actually, I'll have the same."

Dan quirked a brow. "Gonna join me in a little te-kill-ya, eh? Well, why not. It'll help you sleep on the flight."

They took seats on the royal-blue and silver padded bar stools, next to a man who resembled a bad-tempered sea lion. Dan nodded at him, and the man inclined his head. "What's your destination?" His accent identified him as Australian.

"Heathrow."

"You may be delayed, mate. My flight's just been canceled due to inclement weather, and it's by no means the only one."

Dan took a large sip of the margarita delivered to him by the bartender. "That's not good. We did notice that it's foggy out there, but they went ahead and checked us in, took our bags."

The sea lion shrugged. "Perhaps all's well for you, then. Cheers. I'm bloody waiting to see if it'll clear out and I can get on the next flight to Hong Kong."

Lil made a sympathetic noise and put her own margarita glass to her lips, relishing the taste of salt, lime and tequila. Little crystals of salt stuck in the corners of her mouth and she had to lick them off.

"Otherwise," the man continued, "I'll get stuck in a seedy airport hotel overnight."

Dan looked thoughtful, but said nothing. He turned to Lil, smiled and rubbed off a salt crystal she'd missed. Just the touch of his thumb against the corner of her mouth sent a shock of awareness through her, and she wondered how she planned to travel with the man for the next week without, as Shannon would say, jumping his bones.

They chatted idly with the sea lion for the next half-hour, during which Lil discovered that margaritas were as potent as cosmopolitans but tasted even better.

The Australian was a high-level manager for an international bank, married with children and a "vile, stinking ferret" that his wife's "bugger of a stepbrother" had bestowed upon his niece and nephews.

Lil listened politely, burying her smile in her margarita glass and guessing that the sea lion had consumed a couple too many gin and tonics. Really, people ought to learn to hold their liquor so they weren't loud in public.

She peered down at her feet, which were shod in beige Ferragamo sling-backs and seemed very far away. Surely tequila didn't cause one's legs to lengthen?

Dan shot a glance at her and she smiled happily, listening to the absurd taped chirping of the birds in the background. He pushed a bowl of mixed nuts down the bar to her. "Lil, you should eat something."

"No, thank you. I loathe nuts. Little particles stick in your teeth."

"Would you like some olives, then? A sandwich?"

She leaned forward conspiratorially. "Know what I'd really like?"

"What's that?"

"A bowl full of maraschino cherries."

"O-kaay. Would you like a spoon with that?"

She shook her head and whispered, "I like to eat them with my fingers."

Dan's mouth twitched, but he signaled the bartender. "Can we get a small bowl of maraschino cherries for the lady, please?"

The man nodded.

"When I was around eight and met Jane," Lil confessed, "her dad would buy them for me. Once I sliced a bunch of them in half and stuck them on the ends of all my fingers. He called me Miss Cherry Jubilee."

Dan laughed.

"Nana wouldn't buy them. May I have another margarita?"

"Do you think that's a good idea?"

"I think it's an excellent idea." The bartender brought the bowl of cherries and she said thank you. Then she plucked one out of the bowl and dangled it by the stem.

Dan's eyes widened slightly as she held it above her lips and touched it with her tongue, feeling the slick, cold surface. She pulled the cherry from the stem with her teeth and savored it. "Mmm. I love these things."

His Adam's apple moved convulsively as he swallowed. "I can tell."

The wonderful, artificial cherry flavor and about a gallon of chemical red dye burst across her tongue and she smiled. She chased it with more potent, lime-tinged margarita, and enjoyed the tartness of that flavor, too.

Dan's gaze, intent on her face, never wavered. The sea lion continued to pontificate about something and didn't notice that his audience was anything less than rapt.

Dan leaned over and murmured into her ear. "*Now* you look like a lady enjoying herself. There's nothing that gives me such a rush as watching you do that. It's very sexy."

Heat rushed to her cheeks. "Really?" She plucked another cherry from the bowl.

He nodded. "What else do you love, Lil? Besides Krispy Kremes and chocolate tortes?"

She thought about it. "True confession time? I was never allowed to have junk food. And Shannon wasn't, either. When we went to her house, her mom did buy us croissants for breakfast. But when we went to Jane's, her dad would give us those canned SpaghettiOs for lunch."

Dan brightened. "You like SpaghettiOs? My favorite!"

Lil nodded. "And blueberry Pop-Tarts for breakfast. Besides maraschino cherries, there's nothing yummier than a factory-produced, preservative-laden blueberry Pop-Tart."

He laughed.

The sea lion was now describing, to his gin and tonic, the rigors of housebreaking a ferret. The gin and tonic appeared fascinated.

Lil took a third cherry and rubbed it along the rim of her margarita glass, coating its plump, shiny red skin with salt. She bit into it and analyzed the sweet/salty taste before wrinkling her nose, which probably wasn't ladylike.

Dan shook his head at her. "Better with lime, not cherry."

She nodded.

A white-jacketed attendant approached them. "Mr. Granger? Ms. London?"

Dan nodded.

"I'm terribly sorry to inform you that your flight to Heathrow has been canceled due to inclement weather. We can get you on another one, but not until the early morning. In the meantime, I'd be more than happy to assist you in finding accommodations for the night."

Dan frowned and looked a question at Lilia. She supposed she should be irritated at the inconvenience, but she was at the bottom of her second 'rita, as Dan called them, and she just couldn't summon the urge to mind. They were in beautiful surroundings and quite frankly, she wanted to stay here and have another drink.

"Don't you think," she confided to the man in the white jacket, "that Mr. Granger has the most beautiful eyes?"

"Er, quite so, madam."

"And the sexiest mouth."

"Indeed."

Dan cleared his throat. "Lil, you're making me blush, I swear."

"May I have just one more margarita?"

"Right away, madam."

"I'm not sure that's such a hot idea," said Dan.

Lil looked at her feet again, and they had definitely gotten farther away. Another drink would help her reach them, so she could slip off the left shoe, the strap of which had rubbed a raw spot at her heel. "Just one?" she asked.

He sighed. "Just one, then." He turned back to Mr. White Jacket. "I think those accommodations you mentioned might be a real good idea. Thank you."

DAN POURED a giggling, one-shoed Lil through the door of her hotel room an hour and a half later. "Here you are, sweetheart. See, I'm putting your carry-on right here, on the stand. And I'll be right on the other side of that adjoining door."

He looked at her regretfully. Her hair was mussed and she had the sexiest little smear of lipstick mixed with salt crystals at the side of her adorable mouth. He wanted her like hell, but she'd crossed the line from tipsy to pretty much downright drunk an hour ago, and he was man enough not to take advantage of her. She'd expressed her desire to keep things businesslike between them, and while he'd have been happy to change her mind if she were sober, he needed to honor her request since she wasn't.

"You're not going to stay with me?" she looked as if he'd just run over her dog or something.

"I don't think it's a real good idea, Lil. I think you need to eat something besides maraschino cherries. Want me to order you something from room service?"

She shook her head. "No, thank you."

"Okay." He moved to the door. Then he turned. "You sure?"

Lil had whipped off her top, revealing a delicate, lacy, pink silk camisole with the slimmest of spaghetti straps and a low scoop neck. He could see her little pink nipples through the champagne-colored lace, and heat immediately shot to his groin.

"Will you be the mint on my pillow?" she asked shyly, unzipping her skirt. It fell to the floor, revealing that the camisole was in reality a teddy—and a skimpy one, too.

Aw, Christ. His heart leaped out of his chest and impaled itself on his sudden, raging erection. He guessed it was a new kind of heart attack—just as immobilizing as the old kind. Dan forced himself to back slowly toward the connecting door. "Lil," he said unsteadily. "You are not yourself. I want you to go into the bathroom, take two aspirin with some water and lie down. If you still feel this way tomorrow, then I'll be anything you want. But you should get some sleep, because we've got an early wake-up call comin'."

She watched him with sad puppy-dog eyes as he opened the door and backed through it, then closed it again. *Granger, you are nuts. What other man would turn her down, dressed like that?*

He stripped off his clothes and threw himself facedown on the bed in his own room. *Think about politics,* he told himself. *Think about the weather. Think about the kids you'll be hosting at the ranch.* Wild teenage boys, just as he'd been.

But Dan was unable to get her image out of his mind's eye. Worse, he couldn't get himself to relax and fall asleep, because his ears kept pricking, alert for any electric buzzing noise he might hear from Lil's room. Had she brought the Day-Glo orange vibrator with attachments? And was it possible that she was using it on herself, since he hadn't obliged her?

Dan groaned and bit his pillow. Maybe it hadn't been such a brilliant idea to invite Lil along on this trip as his date.

LIL WALKED unsteadily into the bathroom to take the aspirin he'd suggested. She filled a glass with water and glared at herself in the mirror. She looked pretty damned good, if she did say so herself.

"What's wrong with you?" she asked her reflection in the mirror. "Are you going to stop living like a little old lady, or what?"

Dan obviously was used to women who were more sexually adventurous than she. He'd found her easy to turn down, and it was obviously because she hadn't...done what he'd asked her to do the other day. She was boring in bed, a prude.

Prude is one letter away from prune. Prunes are wrinkled and dried up. You never see a prune in anyone's fruit bowl. They're not attractive.

Lil visualized doing what Dan had asked, and heat broke out all over her body like a rash. She clung to the faux marble bathroom counter with one hand, not quite steady on her feet.

She eyed the connecting door between his room and hers. All she had to do was walk to that door and open it. Simple, right?

So she did.

His room was dark except for the blue, flickering light of the television, which was tuned to a blues music station.

He lay on his side, his head supported by one hand, the remote in the other. His eyes widened when he saw her, and he sat up.

"Feel like company?" she asked. "Because the old lady next door might just be ready to explore that, um, option you mentioned the other day."

Dan seemed bereft of speech. Finally he licked his lips and swallowed. The TV began to play Ella Fitzgerald's "People Will Say We're in Love," and Lil hooked the straps of her camisole under her thumbs. She drew them down, over her shoulders, and dropped the entire thing to the floor.

She liked the way it slithered down her body, slipping away like an inhibition and puddling on the floor.

Lil walked to the bed, her hips swaying, and he reached for her, pulling her on top of him. He seemed to be naked under the sheet, and she could feel him hard against her. His mouth found hers and he made love to her lips, his tongue gliding against hers, sweet and hot.

He trailed kisses over her neck and shoulders, raising goose bumps on her skin. He found her nipples and pleasured them, cupping her breasts in his big hands.

She wished that her whole body could fit into his mouth at once, that she could dissolve there on his tongue.

Lil sat astride him as Ella segued into "Be Kind."

This is my first affair... she sang.

Lil stroked Dan's rough jaw, his cheeks, his ears. His hands skimmed over her back, along her spine, leaving what felt like streaks of heat in their wake. And then they moved down to her bottom, which he cupped and squeezed and stroked.

He also moved her inexorably forward, until she was sitting almost on his shoulders. Nervous now, she felt a brief flash of shame as his big hands on her cheeks lifted her and brought her forward. Could she really do this?

She hovered, poised on her knees directly above him. She could feel his hot breath spiraling up, and the sight of his grin below took her breath away.

"Come 'ere, darlin'," he said, and dragged her hips down toward him. She felt unbelievably dirty, doing this, though she told herself rationally that there were far, far filthier things that two—or three or four—human beings could do.

Slowly she let herself sink down and Dan's mouth met her eagerly, his tongue lapping and sliding over her. She couldn't help the small, inhibited scream that came from her throat.

It seemed to excite him, because he found the most sensitive part of her with renewed vigor. Lil reached blindly in front of her and grabbed the edge of the headboard as he plunged his tongue into her and then swirled it around at a spot that made her come sexually unglued. Shame went out the window and there was only sensation, only his mouth and the feel of his hands on her bottom.

Her thighs began to shake uncontrollably and she tried to buck away from him as orgasm hit and shattered any control she had left. But he held her to his mouth with erotic determination and a tender sort of dominion that she'd never known.

Lil spasmed, cried out, spasmed, cried out, trembling and overcome with pleasure. She was wet with it, wild with it and wide-open. She had never, ever experienced anything like this.

He finally released her, judging that she could stand no more, and she collapsed against him, wanting to communicate gratitude but knowing that "thank you" didn't quite cut it.

"You're so beautiful," Dan murmured, "when you allow yourself pleasure. I've never seen anything so gorgeous." He stroked her hair, her shoulders, her back. She ran her hands down his body to find that he was still rock-hard, and she tugged at his shoulder to try to roll him on top of her.

He laughed gently at her efforts, and finally obliged her. "We need a condom, honey," he said, rolling off her seconds later. She waited for him to come back from the bathroom, missing his warmth.

He came back sheathed and lost no time in picking up where they had left off, seeming to delight—as she did—in driving into her with one, sure stroke. Her muscles and nerves tautened with the fast penetration and gloried in it. She began to lose reality again to rhythm and sensation and the smell and texture of his skin. The scents of their bodies had mingled into a joined, male/female essence that combined feral with floral, strength with subtlety.

She rode and he rode, each a cradle for the other's pleasure. The thought crossed her mind that this wasn't civilized English riding at all…she had somehow come to appreciate the Wild West very much indeed.

17

LIL AWOKE to the shrieking of the telephone next to her ear. It was almost as loud as the sledgehammer in her head and the thunderous mortification that hit her next as a sleepy, naked Dan Granger grabbed the phone and muttered into it. He dropped it back into the cradle, scrubbed a hand over his bristly face and sat up, swinging his muscular legs over the edge of the bed.

"Mornin', sleepyhead," he said to her, as if everything were normal and she weren't the Whore of Babylon in a Judith Martin suit.

Dear Miss Manners,
What's the proper way to address the gentleman whose face you've just sat upon?
Signed, Luridly Laid in New York.
Dear Luridly Laid…

Lil couldn't even imagine the response to this. She pulled the covers up over her head.

Dan was so rude as to snatch them down. "Gotta get up, darlin' Lil. We don't want to miss our flight—though now that I see you naked again, I can think of all sorts of creative ways to be late."

She snatched the covers back and pulled them over her face again.

"Are we feeling cranky this morning?"

Nope, we're feeling skanky *this morning.*

She said nothing.

"Does your little head hurt, baby?"

Yes, humiliation and remorse have a harsh sting to them—somewhat like tequila the morning after.

She nodded, still mummified in the bed covers.

"Come on, my little tigress. Let's show our morning stripes!"

Really, could the man be more annoying? He was a professional irritant.

She, on the other hand, was not professional at all. *Professionals don't straddle their client's faces and ride hell for leather, clutching the headboard and howling at the popcorn ceiling like an* American Idol *contestant.*

If Lil had had the remainder of the bottle of tequila, she would gladly have doused herself with it and stuck a lighted match up her left nostril.

Then she wouldn't have to look at the man who was stripping her of the covers yet *again*—much less listen to him.

She discovered that shame actually had a taste: a mixture of lime, stale alcohol and maraschino cherry.

"Okay, princess. Get up." The Beast grabbed one of her wrists and one of her ankles and hauled her off the bed, carrying her into the bathroom, where he settled her unceremoniously onto the toilet!

"I'm sure you have to use that," he said, turning on the shower.

Lil's last remaining shred of dignity fluttered feebly and she shot off the toilet and out of his bathroom, through the connecting door and into her own bathroom.

He had expected her to pee in front of him? Was the man crazy?

She thought about the fact that he dealt with farm animals all the time, and supposed she shouldn't be surprised. But she was not a farm animal! Not today, anyway. She still wasn't sure what sort of creature she'd been last night.

She shuddered.

Then she thought about how hard Shannon would laugh if she could see how angst-ridden Lil was today. She tried to shrug off the angst. So she'd sat on a man's face. Women did it every day, and probably sometimes twice. What was the big deal? Why was she such a Goody-Two-Shoes?

She didn't know. All she knew was that her two shoes did not belong on either side of a man's face while her goodies were in his mouth.

Lil was so upset that she couldn't pee, even though she needed to. She closed her eyes. She was way beyond anal retentive: she was bladder retentive! What would Freud say about that? What would Jane say?

Suddenly she wanted Jane's advice in the worst way. Jane would be calm and rational and get her back to the point where she could indulge in normal bodily functions. She would tell Lil how she should handle this situation.

But how could she possibly call Jane up on her cell phone and discuss something this…private?

She couldn't. And that was all there was to it.

Lil turned on her own shower and tried to scrub away all her confusion and mortification and concerns. She practically shoved the little bar of soap up into her uterus as she agonized over whether she—ugh, ugh, ugh!— might smell down there. Horrible thought.

Something she'd been entirely unconcerned about last night with all the tequila in her. Something she hadn't allowed herself to even wonder before, when she and Dan had done it in the dining room.

Since she couldn't call Jane, she got out of the shower and wrapped herself in a towel and pretended that she was talking to her. Jane would say, "He works with barnyard animals. There is no worse smell. And it's not like he's treating you any differently today, right? You are a woman, these things are natural, and you're being silly."

Right. Thanks, Jane.

Lil got dressed in the spare outfit she'd packed in her carry-on and fastened Nana Lisbeth's pearls around her neck and in her ears. There. Now she at least didn't *look* like the Whore of Babylon. She looked like the conservative businesswoman she had been a week ago, before Dan Granger had strolled into her life and said, "Haaaaaaaaa."

Before he'd turned her life upside down.

A knock sounded on the connecting door. Dan asked, "You okay in there, Lil?"

"I'm just fine, thank you."

"We need to get a move on, darlin'."

"One moment, and I'll be ready." She quickly gathered her things and threw them back into the carry-on which had been carefully organized earlier, everything in its place.

Now she mashed her toiletries, her dirty clothes and the teddy in any which way they would fit. They resembled her thoughts and emotions. She put those out of her mind and zipped the bag closed.

She opened the door.

"Ready?" asked Dan. He leaned forward to kiss her.

She bent quickly to pick up her bag, avoiding the intimacy. "Yes, I'm all set."

He frowned and scanned her face. "How's your head?"

Quite a mess, thank you. She smiled. "A little painful."

"You need aspirin?"

"I'm afraid it will upset my stomach."

He nodded. "Well, we'll get you settled on the plane and give you some hair of the dog."

"I beg your pardon?"

"Hair of the dog that bit you. Tequila. You drink some more, you'll feel better right away."

Oh, I don't think so! I'm never touching the stuff again as long as I live. She gave him a wan smile and he took her bag from her. "You don't have to carry that—"

"Don't forget your pocketbook, Lil."

"Thank you." Unbelievable. She'd been about to walk out of the room without it. What was wrong with her?

SHAME TURNED OUT not only to have a taste but a sedative effect. Lil slept for several hours on the flight to Heathrow, and even when she wasn't sleeping, she pretended to. Dan left her alone except for tucking a blanket around her, which made her feel cherished but confused her even more.

Eventually, though, she had to get up and prepare for their landing in London. She headed for the first-class lavatory, splashed water on her face and repaired her minimal makeup. She wondered what Dan's mother, stepfather and sister would be like. And she looked forward to seeing more of the city whose name she bore.

She made her way back to her seat, where Dan whispered to her how disappointed he was not to have been able to induct her into the Mile High Club. Lil sent him a quelling look.

They made their way off the plane and through customs. They were met in baggage claim by a very thin and otherwise nondescript man in a navy uniform, holding a sign that said Granger.

Mr. Nondescript's name was Ormsby, and he loaded their baggage into the trunk of a black four-door sedan and then navigated them out of Heathrow and into London while they looked around with interest. Ormsby took them on a scenic tour and pointed out some of the sights in his clipped accent, very much like Lil's grandfather Henry's.

They drove past Buckingham Palace with its rows of rigid guards in the famous tall, furry black hats. They saw monumental Big Ben and the lovely Houses of Parliament and the grim, looming Tower of London. They passed Harrod's and many other landmarks, finally pulling up in front of a grand neoclassical house in a chic neighborhood.

Ormsby opened the door for them, Dan discreetly slipped him a folded bill and they mounted the front steps to tap the door-knocker. A middle-aged woman in uniform admitted them, but her polite greeting was cut short when a whoop sounded from the top of the elegant, curved staircase and a high, girlish voice shouted, "Danimal!"

Lil took in a flash of blue and a mop of blond curls as a petite twenty-something girl raced down the stairs, her shoes making a clatter. She bounced as she hit the floor at the bottom and flew into Dan's arms. Lil guessed this must be Claire.

He picked his sister up easily and swung her around, laughing, before he set her down, held her back by the shoulders and scrutinized her. "You haven't changed at all, Clary."

"No, silly, why would I?"

This was the sister who'd asked Dan to go to charm school for her sake? It didn't add up. Especially when she bellowed up the stairs, "Roddy! Get your arse down here to meet my brother!"

The woman in uniform winced.

Another head appeared at the top of the stairs, this

one expensively coiffed, colored and highlighted. Angelic blue eyes wore a permanently disappointed look and gazed down a flawlessly made up nose which shaded once-perfect lips that now sported vertical lines above and below them. The lines radiated outward in a genteel sunburst.

Dan's mother, Lil presumed. Clad in top quality cashmere from neck to ankles, she glided down the staircase while Dan stiffened almost imperceptibly. She offered him her cheek and extended a world-weary hand to Lil.

Dan brushed the woman's face slightly with his lips as heat bloomed in Lil's cheeks. *You shouldn't be kissing your mother with that mouth, cowboy.*

Lil took the woman's cold, dry hand and shook it briefly, saying what a pleasure it was to meet her.

"Likewise, Miss London. I'm Louella Leighton. We're charmed to have you here for the wedding, aren't we, Claire?"

"Yes, absolutely!" Claire put an arm around Lil's shoulders and squeezed. Then she winked at Dan. "Now, how did you two meet?"

Dan and his mother began to speak at the same time. Then he stopped, his expression grimly aware.

"Claire, I told you, love. Dan was in Connecticut on business and met Miss London through mutual acquaintances."

"Yes, that's exactly how it happened," Dan said, fixing his mother with a steely glare that promised they would be chatting later.

Oh, dear. Lilia glanced from one to the other.

Claire ignored the tension and shouted up the stairs again. "Roderick!"

"Darling, how many times must I tell you, use the intercom or that awful cell phone of yours. Do *not* shriek at your fiancé like a banshee." Louella frowned at her daughter. "And don't curse, either. I heard you shout that vulgar word earlier."

"What vulgar word?" Claire asked, looking irritated. "You mean arse?"

Louella cringed. "Please excuse her, Miss London."

"Call me Lil."

"Oh, how pretty." Before Dan's mother could continue, yet another head popped over the banister and looked down curiously, this one a wildly unruly dark one. "What the devil are you making such a racket for, Claire? Oh, is this the famous Lone Ranger brother, then? Halloooo. How d'you do? I'm Roddy, the bloke making off with your sister. Are you here to kick the stuffing out of me, then?"

Mrs. Leighton looked despairing.

Claire laughed.

Dan looked up at him with an inscrutable expression while Roddy stared boldly back. Finally Dan's mouth twitched and he said, "Damn straight I am."

"Language, Daniel!"

"Arse, arse, arse," said Claire.

Lil struggled to keep a straight face while Louella looked daggers at her daughter, who smirked right back at her and then looked mildly repentant. "Sorry, Mum."

A door opened just down the main hall, and a tall

gentleman with regal bearing and the body of a pear emerged. He peered at them as if they were all peasants who hadn't bathed in a few days.

"Nigel!" Mrs. Leighton surged toward him, her hand to her brow. "Daniel and Miss London have arrived, the Stebbenses have just canceled—can you imagine! How boorish—and Mrs. Clapham has pressed the wrong lot of table linens. I feel a migraine coming on."

He blinked at her and then looked instead at his daughter, for whom he had an indulgent smile.

Dan stepped forward and held out his hand. "Hello, Nigel. How are you?"

Nigel took in the elegant cut and expensive fabric of his stepson's jacket, not to mention the quality of his shoes and the genius of his haircut, and blinked again. "Daniel? Is that you?"

"Yes, sir. You're looking well."

Nigel took the proffered hand and pumped it in a slightly wary fashion.

"May I present my date for the wedding, Miz Lilia London? Lilia, my stepfather, Nigel Leighton."

Lovely Nigel—as Lil had come to think of him— took her hand and seemed to decide that she, out of all of them, had bathed. "Delighted to make your acquaintance, my girl. Welcome to Leighton House."

Roddy had finally made it down the stairs and strolled up behind Nigel. A muscle jumped in his cheek at the words *Leighton House* and Lil guessed that it had recently been christened that.

Roddy stuck out his hand toward Dan. "Claire's told me a lot about you."

"Has she? I do hope some of it was good."

"Not a bit," said Roddy with a grin. "She said you were a big brute who'd swing me from the end of a rope if I didn't treat her like a princess, didn't you, Clary?" He looked Dan over while a distressed Louella clutched at the curved banister and Lovely Nigel looked vaguely constipated.

Roddy continued. "And here you are, a big brute as promised. Where's the rope, then?"

Claire laughed.

"In my suitcase," said Dan. "Don't give me an excuse to go get it."

Louella gasped. Lovely Nigel said, "Now see here!"

Roddy laughed. "Well, of *course* I will. Otherwise we'll have no fun at all." He clapped Dan on the shoulder and the two men exchanged a look of amused understanding.

Roddy continued, "I've been waiting a dog's age for my man Nigel, here, to at least clean his gun over an interview in the parlor—but he seems distressingly partial to the idea of me taking his daughter off his hands."

"Nothing to do with the Blackthorne name, Roderick, eh?" Nigel winked. "My daughter could do worse."

Roddy, the amusement dying from his face, shot him a carefully neutral glance. "She could do better, sir. She's quite a catch."

Louella put a fond hand on his arm. "Aren't you sweet."

Roddy looked down at her manicured fingers and stepped away from them to sling an arm around Claire, who wore a fixed smile.

Dan's smile, on the other hand, was becoming quite genuine as he watched the nuances and ugly truths bloom in the foyer of Leighton House. The AristoCat he'd been sent to charm school to impress despised people who were overly conscious of his name and title. He couldn't care less about his status—to the point that he didn't comb his hair. And Dan liked him for it.

Louella, who didn't seem to have noticed the subtle snub dealt to her by her prospective son-in-law, exclaimed that they should all go into the drawing room and have some tea.

Lil settled herself on a chaise longue that looked beautiful but was, in fact, hideously uncomfortable. She watched as Dan handled himself with more grace than anyone in the room.

Louella was far too stiff and formal, Nigel made no effort to keep the conversation flowing and Roddy, though he did make an effort to conceal his dislike of the couple, didn't go out of his way to charm them, either. Claire seemed uncomfortable, torn between her parents and her fiancé.

Dan was nice to everyone. He asked his mother about her dress, Nigel about business, Claire about wedding preparations. He talked about changes in the agricultural industry with Roddy and brought up topics that he knew Lil and Louella could converse about.

He handled his teacup with grace and his food with simple competence. Himself he handled with certainty.

Perhaps she hadn't been able to change his accent, but Lil had grown to love it, and she felt pride swelling within her for Dan. All she'd done was give him a few pointers. The qualities that made him a true prince were all his own: kindness, generosity and intelligence.

Lil was impressed with him, especially since she knew that anger at his mother bubbled underneath his poised surface. The truth had come out: she'd lied to him about it being Claire's idea that he go to Finesse. Claire couldn't care less about Dan's manners. What would he say to Louella later?

_18_

AFTER TEA, Dan and Lilia were shown to their rooms in Leighton House. Louella tried to have the housekeeper do this, but Claire waved her away and took them upstairs herself, after kissing Roddy goodbye. They would see him at the rehearsal dinner that night.

The English didn't do big rehearsal dinners in the American way, but the Leightons were having their out-of-town guests over for drinks and an informal buffet so that they wouldn't be at loose ends for the evening.

Dan cast a glance through the house as they headed for the stairs. He shook his head. The whole place was huge and sparkling with knickknacks. Floral chintz and coordinating stripes and plaids abounded. So did oil portraits of grumpy old men and women who looked as if their hair was pulled too tight.

He saw no signs of a pet to get hair on anything or spread unpleasant odors. In his opinion, the place could use a few dog or cat hairs. It looked like a decorating magazine, and it smelled artificial—as if the whole house had just been carefully unwrapped from cellophane.

His father's old ranch house wasn't too pretty, but at least it was comfortable, smelled like a real home and didn't have a useless object or plastic plant perched on every available surface.

How Claire had grown up here and still retained her natural, bright personality he didn't know.

She led Lilia to her room first, an airy feminine space in lilac and yellow. Then she took Dan to his, a darker, more masculine room with heavy furniture, done in deep greens and burgundies.

"How many bedrooms are in this damned place again?" Dan asked. "It's the size of a hotel."

"Twelve," said Claire. "A bit much for three people, isn't it? And soon they'll be down to two. They won't be able to find each other—but that may suit them."

"Why, are they not getting along?"

"Oh, Danimal. They get along fine—they just don't spend any time together. They lead separate lives." She looked sad. "I do hope that Roddy and I won't end up like them."

"You won't, baby." He pulled her close and gave her a hug. He kissed the top of her blond head. "It's work, I hear, but you can keep your lives intertwined."

She looked up with a grateful smile.

"Nervous?"

"A bit," she admitted.

"He seems like a good guy."

"He is." She scuffed her toe around the rug. "They like him for all the wrong reasons, you know."

"Yes. But you like him for the right ones. That's all that matters. I was ready to hate him—the only thing I knew was that his father had a seat in the House of

Lords and that you wanted me—" He broke off, feeling the anger rise in him again.

"What?"

"Clary, were you worried that your rude cowboy half brother might embarrass you at your wedding?"

Her eyes widened and her jaw slackened. "No. What are you talking about?"

"You never asked Mama to get me into etiquette classes or to change my wardrobe?" He scrutinized her, his jaw tight, but he already knew the answer.

"She *didn't!* She used me to get to you!"

He nodded.

"That explains why you look so different, why you even speak differently. I told Roddy to expect a real cowboy—he's been looking forward! I told him you'd show up in your boots. Instead you're a New Yorker with a Texas accent."

Claire actually kicked the foot of his bed. "Sometimes I really *hate* her. I'm so sorry, Dan."

Dan surprised himself. Instead of agreeing with his little sister, he said, "Don't talk like that, Clary. She may have behaved in an underhanded way, but she did it for you. She didn't want me to mortify you in front of your new family and everyone."

Claire folded her arms across her chest and gazed at him with eyes much older than her twenty-one years. "Mummy was worried about herself, and you know it. She spends more time and energy trying to cover up her background than she does on decorating or living. And the ironic thing is that people find her past fascinating and wish she would talk about it. How she was married to a real cowboy who swept her off her feet and onto a ranch. It's a lot more exciting than being stuffy and sedate and pretentious."

Dan threw back his head and laughed. "They want to know about Dad?"

"Yes! And I think Father has a giant complex about him. That's why we weren't allowed to visit much, you know."

"No, I didn't know." The idea of Lovely Nigel being intimidated by his poor old dad was difficult for Dan to wrap his mind around. "She never even asks about Dad."

"She's dreadful."

"Clary, don't talk about her like that. She loves you. She's your mother, for all her faults. You owe her some respect." He couldn't believe the words were coming out of his mouth. But just because he had a dysfunctional relationship with Louella didn't mean that Claire should.

"I can't believe you're sticking up for her like this, after she lied to you and manipulated you."

He shrugged and ran a hand through his hair. "What're you gonna do, Claire? Nobody gets to choose his mother. Just like mothers don't get to choose their children. Sometimes it's a bad match, but it's the only match we got. Know what I mean? You may as well love the parts of her that are lovable. And she's got some. Remember the Mickey Mouse hotcakes she'd make? And how she'd put green food coloring in the milk on St. Patty's Day?"

Claire grinned. "Yes. She was great when we were

small, wasn't she? Did she make you elaborate birthday cakes?"

He nodded.

"I will never forget the castle cake she made when I turned thirteen. Turrets, flags, a drawbridge and a moat! A work of art."

"She hasn't made your wedding cake, has she?"

Claire laughed. "No, but I think she wanted to try her hand. She settled for driving the pastry chefs mad."

She took his hands and squeezed them. "Did you bring your boots, Danimal?"

"Would I travel without them?" He smiled down at her.

"Then I want you to wear them to my wedding."

"You what? I can't do that. Mama will have my head, and Lil told me never, ever to—"

"Will you wear them as a personal favor to me? With a bolo string tie?"

He looked down into her fresh, flushed face, the big blue eyes pleading with him not to change for her. How he loved his baby sister. "Yeah."

"Stetson, too?"

"I didn't bring it. But I do have a couple of gag gifts for you and Roddy that you can open tonight." He was glad he hadn't let Lilia talk him out of leaving them behind.

"Excellent! Now, why would Lilia—who seems very sweet, by the way—forbid you to do anything? She's not a general, she's your girlfriend."

"She's not my—" Dan shut his mouth. It sure would be nice if she'd be his girlfriend.

"I can tell by the way she looks at you that she loves you."

"Say what? Bull. Claire, Lil is my, um, etiquette consultant." *Damn, does that sound lame or what?* "I wouldn't even know her, if Mama hadn't tricked me."

"Your etiquette consultant? You mean you paid her to come with you?" Claire looked upset.

He nodded. "I mean, I'd like her to be more than that, but we're still figuring that part out, if you know what I mean."

"I don't know what to say. Honestly, I don't." Claire moved to the door. "Just promise me that you won't let her change you in any way that counts. I don't care if you use the right fork at tomorrow's banquet."

"I do," Dan said quietly. "I'm still your brother, honey. But I don't want anyone to have to apologize for me. Not ever again. And if Lil can help me accomplish that, she is worth her weight in gold."

LIL WAS WORTH her weight in gold in a hundred other ways, too, Dan reflected as he escorted her downstairs for drinks and dinner. She looked gorgeous tonight in a red silk cocktail dress with an asymmetrical neckline, and pearls that glowed against her warm, honey-colored skin.

She had legs to die for, and he tried not to think of them wrapped around him, as it was neither the time nor the place.

He himself wore a dark suit with a silk tie and a snowy-white shirt. His shoes and his manners were polished to perfection. Lil had nodded with approval upon seeing him, but she seemed subdued—sad?—for some reason.

"You feeling all right?" Dan asked her.

"I'm fine," she said. "Just a little jet-lagged, thanks."

She'd seemed stiff and formal ever since they'd woken up together, and he didn't think it was due to jet-lag. But he didn't press her.

The housekeeper, Mrs. Winger, led them to a grand reception room at the back of the house, where French doors had been thrown open to an elegant, covered back porch and carefully tended gardens surrounding a fountain.

Louella and Nigel were already there and a maid inquired as to what they'd all like to drink.

Dan placed his two wrapped packages on a low table. At his mother's raised brow, he explained. "Just a couple of small gifts for the happy couple."

Louella was dressed in royal-blue, and Nigel in a dark suit much like his own. They chit-chatted until the maid came back in with a large tray. She'd brought their drinks, but also a large pitcher with margarita glasses. Dan stared at it in disbelief, while next to him, Lil stiffened.

"Your sister, Daniel, requested that we serve Texas margaritas in your honor," Mama said through a painfully bright smile. Nigel grunted with disapproval.

"How thoughtful of her," Dan said, his lips twitching. There was obviously a domestic skirmish going on behind the scenes, and Claire had just won this round. He turned to Lil. "Margarita for you, darlin'?"

Her beautiful black eyes snapped at him, and her color rose. "No, thank you."

She seemed wooden, almost a caricature of the Miss Manners he'd first met in her Connecticut office. The warmth, wit and sexiness that he'd seen begin to blossom in her was nowhere to be seen. Had he failed some test of hers without even knowing it? Dan's jaw tightened, but he tamped down the stirrings of anger. This was neither the time, nor the place for that, either.

As the guests began to arrive, he was half gratified, half irritated when Mama went out of her way to introduce him as her "marvelously successful rancher son from Texas," and gush about how proud she was of him.

She'd certainly never told anyone she was proud of him when he'd worn scuffed boots, jeans and T-shirts. But now that he sported a thousand-dollar suit, she adored him.

He told himself he was being irrational. Wasn't this what he'd wanted? To force her to acknowledge him? To stand tall in her eyes? Why was the taste of victory so bitter?

Lil mingled easily with every guest, knowing just the right thing to say and charming everyone she met. She was charming to him, too. Yet she treated him with the same amount of politeness that she treated these total strangers. His anger at her grew.

How could she hold him at arm's length after the things they'd experienced together? After she'd thrashed and whimpered in his bed? After he'd been inside her and all over her?

The maid brought out a gorgeous cheese tray, a sliced fruit tray, a platter of pâtés. Then, looking around nervously, she brought out a huge plate of…*nachos?*

He had to be seeing things. Dan looked down at his drink, wondering if someone had slipped something into it. But no, those were big, fat, greasy nachos dotted with plenty of jalapeños, on a silver plate that looked as if it had been in Lovely Nigel's family for generations.

He glanced at his mother's face, which had begun to mottle with fury. The poor maid dodged her and ran— almost bumping into Claire and Roddy as they made their entrance to the party.

Everyone clapped and toasted them. Claire wore an angelic blue dress, discreet diamond earrings and a devilish expression. She winked at Dan and smiled when she saw the margarita pitcher and nachos. He shook his head at her.

Lil glided up and murmured, "I think the entrance of the Tex-Mex food has just instigated World War III."

"I'm afraid you may be right." Dan took her elbow and skimmed her back lightly with his fingers. She shivered but stiffened and then moved away.

"What's wrong, Lil?"

She smiled that polite smile of hers. "Nothing at all. Why?" She smoothed the skirt of her dress unconsciously.

"Do you regret coming?"

"Why on earth would you ask me that? I'm having a lovely time—though the mother-daughter feud is a little worrisome."

He wasn't going to get beyond her social facade.

That much was clear. His anger grew even more. Why was she making herself unavailable to him?

Suddenly he knew the answer. Her job was almost finished. She'd had her fun with him, but the time was fast approaching when they'd part ways—and she had no intention of seeing him again because he wasn't refined enough for her. She'd taught him to fake it. But she'd seen the raw material, and just like his mother she rejected that.

He wasn't good enough for Miz Lilia London, and she was letting him know that, in her ever-so-polite way.

Dan didn't try to touch her again. What was the point? She was only here earning a paycheck, making sure the monkey didn't fart at the dinner table or swing from the chandelier. How could he have thought there might be anything else between them?

Dan avoided talking to Lilia as much as he could for the rest of the evening, only attending to her as much as etiquette required of him.

He sat next to her at dinner, but conversed mostly with the lady on his other side. He stood up after dessert and made an articulate and heartfelt toast to Claire and Roddy. And he laughed as loud as anyone when they opened his gag gifts.

Roddy, the supposedly stuffy aristocrat, blinked twice in shock at the baby-blue Western belt that said, Groom. Then he chortled and donned it with his suit trousers while his father the viscount shouted with mirth. Claire put hers on over her dress, a pink belt that said, Bride. Then they posed for pictures.

Dan turned toward Lil, delighted with the success of his gifts and wanting to share the moment. But she was occupied with the gentleman on the other side of her, and he belatedly remembered his anger. Share the joke with Lil?

He was a fool. He knew better than to fall for the Audrey Hepburns of the world. They always wound up with the Cary Grants, not cowboys like him.

DAN EXCUSED HIMSELF to find the facilities and get a handle on his suddenly dark mood. From what he remembered of his boyhood visit to Leighton House, he knew there was a half-bath near the big, industrially equipped kitchen.

He stepped out of it a couple of minutes later to hear his mother's voice, berating someone. "I don't care what Claire told you to do, Maria! I'll thank you to recall that Claire is not the mistress of this household. *I am!* And I did not sanction that a vile platter of greasy nachos should be brought out to my guests. I am furious, do you hear! In fact, once this evening is over, I'd like you to gather your things and take yourself off. Don't bother to return."

Dan sighed and rounded the corner into the kitchen, where Maria, the maid, was sobbing. This was really his fault. If he hadn't let the cat out of the bag to Claire, she wouldn't have directed Maria to serve the nachos.

"Mama, you shouldn't take this out on Maria."

She whirled and stared at him. "Daniel, this is not your business."

"Unfortunately it is my business, Mama. I asked Claire about whether sending me to Finesse was her idea. She denied all knowledge of it and was quite angry that you'd manipulated me, using her as an excuse. *You lied to me.*"

Louella cast a frantic look in the maid's direction. "I'll thank you, Daniel, not to discuss this in front of the servants!"

He lost his temper. "I'll discuss this in front of anyone I wish, even your fancy guests out there. And you know what? Maria isn't just a servant. She's a *person,* someone with feelings." He turned toward the maid. "Look, darlin', how about I help you find a new place? If not here, then somewhere else. How'd you like to come live in Texas for a while? See the Wild West?"

Her eyes widened in disbelief and then the beginnings of a smile dawned through her tears.

Louella emitted a genteel snarl. "Don't reward her for her part in this!"

"Don't punish her for following orders!" He pulled his wallet out of his back pocket and retrieved a business card. "I'm working on puttin' together a retreat program on my ranch for at-risk boys. We will need someone to help with meals and linens and cleaning. If you're interested, you get in touch, all right? I'd pay your round-trip flight, room, board and a wage."

Louella glowered at her as Maria accepted the card. "Don't think you'll get a reference from me, young lady," she said in a voice shaking with rage.

"She don't need your reference, Mama. Go on, get

outta here, Maria. God forbid my mother should lift a finger to clean up after her own party. We'll manage without you."

·"How dare you, Daniel?"

"How dare *you,* Mama? Over the years you've gone from misguided to stuck up and dishonest and now you're verging on becoming just plain mean. Take a good look at yourself and cut it out before it's too late. You want to be one of those nasty old ladies with a face like a sphincter? The ones who can't wish anything nice for anyone?"

She opened her mouth and gaped at him like a guppy.

"You left Dad and me for a more glamorous lifestyle. You've always been embarrassed about your past, and me because I'm part of that past. But because you couldn't erase me, because Claire and I happen to love each other, you thought you'd polish me up and let me think it was *her* who was embarrassed. I don't know why I didn't figure it out from the get-go.

"It's always about *you,* Mama! You didn't think about the wreck of a man you left behind. You never thought to worry that your son and your husband might have needed you."

"That's not true! I felt awful—"

He held up a hand. "You know, this has all been water under the bridge for years, now. There's no point in discussing it. But I do want to discuss your lying and scheming and manipulating."

"Daniel, it was for your own good—"

"Bullshit! You sending me to Finesse had nothing to

do with my own good, and I won't tolerate you saying so. You're my mother and I'll always love you, but you either apologize to me right now, or I will leave after the wedding tomorrow and never speak to you again. Do you hear me?"

She stared at him.

"I'm done being your disappointing son. The one that needs fixing before you can love him. The one that needs charm school or new clothes or a job that don't require him to get dirty.

"I'm *done*. D'you hear me?"

For a moment his only response was a stricken silence. Then tears formed in Louella's eyes and she swallowed hard.

He watched her almost impersonally as she tried to find the words, as she struggled for what was left of her spirit under all the pretense and denial. He was actually surprised when she did.

"I'm sorry, Danny."

That should have been enough, but it wasn't.

"You've made me feel like shit all these years," he said. "Like I'm not good enough. Well, maybe the truth is that a person of your character ain't good enough for *me*."

She stared at him, her mouth working.

He stared right back.

"I'm so sorry," she whispered.

"Yeah? Well I'm glad you're sorry." He turned his head away from her, knowing he should find some grace and put his arms around her and give her a hug, but he just couldn't. "Thank you for the apology."

She nodded, unable to speak.

"Now I'm going back out there to have me one of those margaritas you've served 'in my honor.' And I'm having some of those nachos, too, because they sure beat the hell outta cucumber sandwiches and stinky Stilton."

19

THE DAY OF the wedding dawned bright and sunny. As Lil understood things, it was Roddy's father who'd made it possible for the wedding ceremony to be held in the famous, spectacular St. Paul's Cathedral. Architect Christopher Wren's masterpiece and burial site of Lord Nelson, the Cathedral stood three hundred fifty-six feet high at the summit of Ludgate Hill. Directly across the Thames the Tate Gallery and the Globe Theatre were visible.

Lil sat with an uncharacteristically quiet Dan in one of the front pews, and smiled at the irony: the man who'd been an impossible country bumpkin was responsible for taking her to the most elegant occasion she'd ever experienced.

She looked fondly at him when she knew he wouldn't notice. He looked incredible in his gorgeously cut tuxedo of the finest, lightweight, black wool. She didn't approve of the black dress Western boots on his feet, but how could he have refused the bride's request? And the bolo string tie became him; it really did.

Louella had taken one look at him and emitted a small shriek. He'd gazed at her calmly, turned his hands palm-up and shrugged. "Claire specially asked me, to, Mama. What d'you want me to do?"

Lovely Nigel shut his eyes against the preposterous sight.

Lil touched their shoulders and said gently, "Pretend he's a Scotsman, wearing the ceremonial kilt. Same thing, really. Texas is its own country. And the president has made cowboy-style quite chic. I attended the Inaugural Ball, you know."

Louella and Nigel relaxed, and wanted to know all about the Ball…

Now the ceremonial music began, and the last stragglers among the guests were hurried in on the arms of the attendants.

The nave of St. Paul's was enormous, but somehow guests filled it almost to capacity, along with candles and flowers. Almost every woman wore a lovely hat, the array of jewels was breathtaking and the architecture of the cathedral, of course, was simply unrivaled. Lil would never forget this wedding.

The wedding march began and she and Dan stood up along with everyone else in the church. They all turned in anticipation of the bride's entrance.

Claire looked exquisite, a glowing, rounder-faced Princess Di, though her dress was very different from the royal princess's. The white gown was tailored to her body, simple and stunning, with pearls sewn around the sweetheart neckline. More pearls dangled from her ears.

But her smile was the only adornment she needed, and it lit St. Paul's even from behind her veil.

At the altar, Roddy's hair was combed neatly for once and he looked euphoric, utterly certain that Claire was the woman of his dreams.

Lil got misty-eyed just looking at them. Dan actually dashed a tear away from his cheek. She wanted to squeeze his arm, rub his back…but a tension had been growing between them and touching him in that way didn't seem appropriate right now.

She watched another tear roll toward his macho, sexy, irreverent cowboy mouth, and he dashed this one away, too—along with her last delusion that she hadn't fallen completely and utterly in love with the man.

Oh, dear God, no. Lil, you're hopeless. He is so wrong for you.

Tears of confusion and self-recrimination formed in her own eyes and rolled down her cheeks. Lil adjusted her hat and dug for a tissue, finding Dan's hand extended with a clean handkerchief instead. That made her want to bawl even more.

Grateful that the ceremony gave her a valid excuse to cry, she allowed herself to indulge a little before she got control over herself.

Now you stop that, young lady. Nana's voice echoed in her ear, and following patterns of the past, she listened.

The service was excruciatingly formal, the language old-fashioned as befit a wedding in St. Paul's. Lil found it lovely and wondered what sort of good luck charm Claire had sewn into the hem of her dress, in the English tradition.

And then all too soon it was over, the vows and

rings exchanged. Roddy and Claire were husband and wife, and exited the church bound for a new life together, starting with their wedding reception in the grand ballroom of Blackthorne House, his ancestral town home.

Blackthorne House was larger than Leighton House but somehow less imposing. It was also a great deal more shabby-chic, though pains had obviously been taken to decorate the ballroom itself.

It was obvious that the Blackthornes had a great many dogs, even though they weren't present for the festivities. For the house, though clean, was full of Eau de Canine. Lil smiled and wondered what breeds they were. She thought, in fact, that when she returned to Connecticut, she'd like not only a dog, but also a cat.

Nana Lisbeth hadn't been able to abide animals in the house, but Lil was tired of living entirely alone. And unlike Claire, she didn't think she'd be getting married anytime soon. She smiled wistfully.

A brief vision of herself, walking in a long white dress toward Dan Granger, popped into her mind. He wore exactly what he wore right this minute: a tuxedo with boots and a bolo tie.

"Can I get you something to drink, Miz Lil?" he asked her, interrupting her silly fantasy.

"That would be lovely, Dan. Thank you. Champagne, please?"

He nodded and made his way toward a circulating waiter with a tray. His broad shoulders were set off to perfection in the dark wool of the tuxedo, and no man

had ever filled out formal slacks the way he did. She fixated on his backside as if it were a particularly delecta-
ble appetizer, and blushed as he turned with two flutes
of champagne and caught her in the act.

He raised a sardonic brow at her.

She suddenly found the orchestra fascinating.

"Your bubbly, darlin'." He loomed over her, extend-
ing the glass, and suddenly her hormones rushed to the
surface like the tiny bubbles in the flute.

Lil thanked him, accepted the glass and took a quick
sip. Her hormones did not belong at Claire's formal
British wedding reception.

"Once Claire and Roddy have shown up and taken
the floor, I do hope you'll honor me with a dance."

She hesitated. *Dance with the man and you'll only
be torturing yourself, you dimwit.* But it was rude to refuse. "Of course," she said.

His mouth twisted. "Well, I wouldn't want you to put
yourself to any trouble, now, Lil. But I figured that we
could show off what we practiced with that French fruit
loop, ya know."

She'd offended him. "Dan, I didn't mean—"

"I know what you meant," he said coldly. "Don't
worry about it." And he turned on his boot-heel and
walked away. She stared after him, miserable, while he
found another woman to talk to almost immediately.

It's for the best, Lil. It really is.

DAN DANCED flawlessly with several other women,
while Lil chitchatted with various guests and tried to

pretend she wasn't watching him covertly. How had she gotten herself into this mess?

And why did he seem so angry? He'd told her, days before, that he could take no for an answer. And he had. Pretty gracefully. So what exactly was his problem now?

She knew what *her* problem was. And she needed to solve it by…by…removing her silly, unpredictable, unmanageable heart and dropping it into the punch bowl.

Lil turned from a conversation at a light touch on her arm. A hopeful gentleman was asking her to dance with him. Though she'd rather have told him to go away, she smiled with every pretense of delight and accepted, moving out onto the dance floor with him in a waltz.

A quick glance around told her that Dan, to her relief, was not there. Lil tried to focus on what the gentleman was saying to her, and did not enjoy his hot, sweaty hand on her lower back, nor the sticky, warm fingers clasped with hers.

She also didn't appreciate the way he leered at her, looking as if he'd like to lick her like a lollipop.

She'd turned her head to avoid his whiskey breath when a large, tanned, scarred hand tapped her repulsive gentleman on the shoulder. Before she knew it, he'd ceded her to Granger.

Dan pulled her closer than he should and glowered down at her. "How am I doin', Teach?"

She looked up and faltered. "F-fine. Why?"

"Because I just live for your approval, darlin' Lil. And I'm not feelin' it much these days."

"I don't know what you mean."

"Of course not. It wouldn't be polite for you to know what I mean. Therefore you play ignorant so you can avoid hurting my feelings, which, after all, would be rude."

"What are you talking a—"

"Lemme ask you a question, Miz London. Is it proper etiquette to let a man take down your drawers and do all manner of hot, naughty, intimate things to you—"

"Keep your voice down!" she hissed, appalled. She tried to pull away, but he held her tight.

"—and then treat him like a dog afterward? Behave as if he's somebody you just asked for the correct time?"

"I haven't treated you that way!"

"You have," he said, his face only an inch away from her burning one.

She tried to pull away again, but he shook his head.

"I guess you've put me in my place, then, Miss Manners. I'm good enough to go down on you, but I ain't good enough for you to socialize with."

"That is ridiculous! I can't believe you just said that, and I'm not going to dignify it with an answer." Furious and mortified, she threw etiquette to the four winds and tore out of his grasp. Then she stalked away from him, leaving him to look foolish on the dance floor in front of five hundred people.

She flew to a double-doored exit and into a convenient powder room, where she locked the door and hyperventilated. Her face was dark red and her whole body trembled with emotion: horror, shame and rage.

She wanted to splash water on her face, but that would destroy her careful makeup. She settled for run-

ning cold water over her hands, which clenched and un-
clenched involuntarily.

*I'm good enough to go down on you but not good
enough to socialize with...*

How could he possibly think that of her? How could
he have said that *in public?* Someone could easily have
overheard him! Loathsome, horrid man. She should
have slapped his rude, mocking face.

And she'd thought herself in love with him? She
didn't love Dan Granger! She despised him.

The cold water and the privacy eventually helped
her calm down. She was going to have to leave the powder room at some point and make it through the rest of
the evening.

No—that wasn't true. She'd made her appearance,
and now she could catch a cab and go back to Leighton
House. The housekeeper would let her in. She could re-
tire to her bedroom there and not have to see Dan again.
She could arrange a separate flight and just send him
a bill.

Armed with this plan, Lil unlocked the door and
stepped outside the little room. To the right, she saw
through a set of French doors that the orchestra was outside taking a break. Several of them were smoking cig-
arettes. She wondered if one of them had a cell phone
and could call a taxi for her. No, better to find her way
to the front of Blackthorne House and request that the
butler do so.

Lil turned toward the left and froze.

Dan lounged casually against the wall. He'd been

waiting for her to come out all this time. "We need to chat, darlin'."

She raised her chin and narrowed her eyes at him, hating the fact that her knees had started shaking again. "We have nothing to chat about."

"You're here on my payroll, and I say we do," he growled. "Besides, it's bad manners to refuse to talk to me."

."Mr. Granger," she said icily, "First of all, I quit. And second, forcing your attentions on a lady is the worst breach of etiquette you can commit. So might I suggest that you *get out of my way* so that I can call a cab? I don't wish to spend *one more second* in your company." She almost added, "you obnoxious son of a bitch," but stopped herself just in time.

"I'll get out of your way when I'm damned good and ready. Did I force my attentions on you when you sat on my face? Was giving you multiple orgasms forcing my attentions on you? As I recall, you begged for my attentions, and couldn't get enough of them."

Her hand came up involuntarily to slap him but he blocked it.

"Is it good manners, darlin' Lil, to drive a man crazy, make him fall in love with you and then decide he ain't fit to lick your stiletto?"

"I never decided any such thing!" she shouted. "That is your own complex and your own set of problems with your mother. All I did was get embarrassed about losing my inhibitions around you, and then top it off by falling in love with you, you big stupid cowpoke! And then I didn't know what to do about it! So *move*," she bellowed, surprised at the force of her own lungs. "Because I hate you and I never want to see you again!"

When he just stood there and stared at her, she lost it completely and started beating him with the only thing she had available: her evening bag. "Move!" *Thwack.*

He opened his big, dumb mouth.

"Move!" she shrieked again. *Thwack! Thwack! Thwack!*

"Lil—"

Thwack! Thwack!

The clatter of heels sounded behind them and a beyond-furious Louella appeared. "Not another word out of either one of you!"

"Butt out, Mama."

"I will *not!* You are being broadcast into the bloody *ballroom!* I will *never, ever, ever* live this down!" And Louella pushed past them and pounced on a cluster of clip-on microphones that they hadn't seen on a side table. Clip-on mikes that the musicians had taken off before going outside for their break.

Lil let out a horrified squeak and stumbled against the wall, using it to remain upright. Her heart thundered in her ears and shame hit her like a baby grand dropped from several stories high.

The entire ballroom had heard them. The entire ballroom. *Did I force my attentions on you when you sat on my face?*

Dan threw back his head and laughed, long and hard. It was a true Texas guffaw in every sense of the word.

His mother, beside herself, slapped his face. Then she turned on her heel and left.

It was all just too much. Lil, always calm, cool and collected in any social situation, burst into tears.

20

Dan was at her side in an instant, his strong arms going around her. "Aw, honey," he said, "don't cry. Things are gonna be fine."

His shirt smelled of starch and the vaguest hint of cologne. It also smelled like him. Part of her wanted to run her hands up underneath it to feel his bare chest beneath. Part of her wanted to grab him by it and shake him until his teeth rattled. She was so utterly confused, furious, mortified.

He produced the handkerchief again and kissed the top of her head. She honked into the square of cloth, stepped away from him and saw that she'd left a large, black mascara blotch on the formerly snowy shirt. She burst into fresh tears. "I'm sorry I ruined your shirt. And I hate you."

He tilted up her chin. "You sure about that? 'Cuz I coulda sworn you just said you'd fallen in love with me."

She shook her head.

"You callin' me deaf as well as stupid?"

This time she nodded.

"Are we both deaf, then?"

She said nothing, just occupied herself with the handkerchief.

"Because I do believe I admitted falling in love with you, too. And I can't even ask you not to tell anyone, because the whole dang ballroom heard me say it."

She blew her nose. The man she hated was in love with her? The man who'd just disgraced her publicly in front of the crème de la crème of London society? Lil slid down the wall, plopped inelegantly onto her bottom and stared at him.

Dan said kindly, "It's socially correct in these situations to say, 'I love you, too.'"

She didn't trust herself to speak.

"Even if it's a little white lie. Remember, you're supposed to lie in certain situations. This etiquette consultant I met once taught me that."

Finally she said, "How can I hate you and love you at the same time?"

He scratched his head. "I don't know. But you can. It's part of the feminine mystique. You gals are all kinda squirrely in the head. Otherwise you'd have kicked us men outta your lives a long time ago. Formed your own planet and just kept us in cages for reproductive purposes."

Lil began to laugh weakly.

"Wait a minute," said Dan. "Did you just admit that you love me?"

She nodded.

"I hear tell that it's customary for two people to kiss after they say that."

"Emily Post, page five hundred ninety-two."

He bent and took her hands, pulling her to her feet. "Lil, darlin', where have you been all my life?" And before she could answer, that sexy cowboy mouth came down on hers.

She fell headlong into the kiss, craving the warmth and the taste and the smell of him. He pulled her so hard against him that they almost fused together, and before she knew it, he was backing her toward the powder room again.

"No!" she said into his mouth, but he ate the word and swallowed it, somehow managing to kiss her and grin at the same time. When he finally raised his head, they were inside and he was kicking the door closed with one of those black boots of his.

"We cannot do this at your sister's wedding!"

He lifted her onto the marble countertop and waggled his eyebrows at her.

"No."

He brushed his thumbs over her nipples and she gasped as sexual lightning streaked through her.

"No?" His hands crept up under her skirt and found the thigh-high stockings held in place by garter straps. "What's this? Oh, God! I promise I won't do anything you don't want me to—just let me see."

His plea was so heartfelt that she couldn't refuse him. She let him lift the skirt of her dress and look with awe at the skimpy red lace garter belt that she wore, for the first time in her life, with one of those "slutty" thongs.

Dan made a desperate, groaning sound and dropped to his knees, clutching his heart. "Matching bra?"

She nodded. "Push up. See-through."

"Show me?"

She couldn't just take off her dress at his sister's wedding! For all she knew, the queen herself could be out there in the ballroom now.

"Please?"

She wavered. "No touching. *Promise*."

"Cruel, cruel woman. I won't touch."

Lil slid off the counter, feeling wicked, and presented her back to him. He eased the zipper down and she stepped out of the blue silk dress, still turned away from him.

In the mirror, she saw Dan actually shove his knuckles into his mouth and gnaw. He moaned past them and feasted his eyes on her.

She turned, looked at him over her shoulder and smiled.

"I'm the scarlet harlot, am I not?"

He shook his head.

The smile fell off her face. "How come?"

"You're just not harlot material, honey. But you are the embodiment of all my fantasies."

"Really?" She couldn't help the pleasure seeping through her veins at his statement. She didn't think she'd ever been a man's fantasy before.

Dan stood up. "I know I promised not to touch, but your strap, there, needs a small adjustment."

"Where?"

"I'll show you." He took two steps toward her, and before she knew what he was about, he'd pulled the left bra strap off her shoulder, the lacy cup down and fastened his mouth over her nipple.

"Ohhh!" The suction was exquisite, the heat wonderful, his tongue irresistible. Lil sagged against him, the big, fat liar.

He chuckled, pulling the strap from her right shoulder off, and that cup down, too.

"You—ahhhh…"

Suddenly the cold, marble counter was beneath her almost bare bottom again and Dan was between her knees while she leaned weakly against the ornate gilt mirror. He slid the thong aside easily and stroked her while she quivered and moaned at his touch.

She shouldn't…he shouldn't…they shouldn't. But as Lil gave in to pleasure, she didn't care if Prince Charles and the Duchess Camilla were out there. All she cared about were Dan's hands on her, and then Dan sliding into her, and finally Dan blurring into a rainbow cowboy who rode her to nirvana.

HE DIDN'T WANT HER to get dressed, but she drew the line at leaving the wedding of the season naked. "Just go call a cab," she urged him. "Then we'll slip out the back."

He set his hands on his hips. "It would be incredibly rude to leave without saying goodbye to Claire and Roddy. You, of all people, should know that."

Lil stepped into her dress and turned so he could zip her up. Her head throbbed at even the thought of entering that ballroom again after they'd been broadcast news. She made an executive etiquette decision. "I don't care."

"Excuse me?"

"I. Don't. Care."

"You don't care about being rude, or you just care too much about what all those bejeweled snobs out there think of you? I think it's the latter."

Lil turned and faced him, her mouth tight. "You ask any other woman in the world if she'd go back into that ballroom with you. The answer will be *no*."

"I didn't ask any other woman in the world. I'm asking you."

"You're absolutely out of your mind."

"No, I'm not. Lil, you've led your entire life trying to impress other people with your manners and letting yourself get lost inside the giant book of etiquette. Your spirit has gotten flattened between the pages. Your soul has become rectangular and bound. I want to see you get the hell outta there! Now take my hand, come back into that ballroom with me, and hold your head high. Show 'em what you've got."

She shrank back from him. "Dan, no! Why are you asking this of me? Why do you want to humiliate me in front of all those people?"

He sighed. "Darlin', I don't want to humiliate you. I want to free you. Don't you see?"

"No, I don't. I'm not doing it."

He took her lightly by the shoulders. "You think those people in there have never had sex?" He looked thoughtful for a moment.

"What does that have to do with—"

"It *is* possible that the English are too repressed to screw. And how do they keep a stiff upper lip while going down on each other? I guess they don't do that, either—"

"Dan!"

"Yes?"

"You need to get over this problem of yours with the English. Because I like your sister and you're going to have to bring me here a lot."

"Is that so?"

"That *is* so."

"Well, I'm not taking you anywhere unless you tilt that little pointed chin up and come dance with me in that ballroom."

"Dan!"

"I guaran-damn-tee you that everyone in there has had oral sex and doesn't give a rat's ass whether you sat on my face or not. Now come on." He took her hand and pulled her to the door.

"Wait. At least let me fix my makeup."

"You are such a girl. I love that about you."

LIL'S KNEES knocked together with every inexorable step to the ballroom. She *so* did not want to go in there.

She considered making a break for it and trying to drown herself in the champagne fountain. But Dan would simply pull her out by her pearls and then make her go in dripping wet.

Speaking of her pearls, perhaps she could take a flying leap and hang herself by them from one of the chandeliers. No—they would break, and Nana Lisbeth would haunt her forever for trying to use her inheritance in pursuit of suicide.

Her last option was to whip off a shoe and use the

spike heel to commit hara kiri right there in the foyer. But she was sure that among the distinguished guests there was a doctor in the house. She'd only be resuscitated in the end.

They got closer and closer to the door.

Dan squeezed her hand and shot her a reassuring glance. "It's gonna be fine, honey."

They walked through the doors and down the shallow steps into the ballroom, only to have all conversation cease while people stared openly at them. The blood drained from Lil's face as even the orchestra stopped.

At a look from Claire they began to play again immediately, and Dan swung Lil out onto the dance floor, supporting her entire weight because her legs had turned to rubber.

The buzz and hum of conversation started again around the room, but Lil had gone too far down the path of humiliation to feel relief. Out of the corner of her eye she saw Claire cross the room to speak to the orchestra. What fresh hell now?

Suddenly the musicians segued into an infectious Texas Two-Step, and Dan's chuckle rumbled in her ear as he moved them into it with gusto. She'd never done it in her life, but it was easy to follow his lead.

Taking their cue from Claire, all of the guests began to clap in time with the music. Bewildered, Lil could only stare at them, these crazy English.

From a back corner of the room, Louella hauled Lovely Nigel onto the dance floor and proceeded to teach him the Two-Step, too. To Lil's surprise, Dan's mother had flair, and she could move her hips like nobody's business.

Lil started to laugh; she couldn't help it. Dan grinned down at her while Roddy, Claire and several other adventurous couples took to the floor with them and carefully copied their movements.

The formal ball was degenerating—or maybe improving—into a Texas hoedown.

Lil found the strength in her legs again and enjoyed it, the feel of Dan's arm around her waist and his hand in hers; the easy rhythm of the dance and the love shining down from his eyes. There was something else there, too…and she realized it was a mixture of pride and respect.

All she'd done was follow him across a threshold and step onto a dance floor. But she had really impressed him along the way.

The song began to wind down, and Dan squeezed the last few steps from the music before dipping her against his arm. Then he brought her back up and kissed her deeply in front of all the English, who surprised them again by breaking into huge applause.

21

THE STEEPLECHASE was to be held in the countryside about an hour from London, at the house of a cousin of Lovely Nigel's.

Roddy was overheard to say that he thought it ridiculous to be transporting all the wedding guests out there when the poor sods simply wanted to nurse their hangovers from the night before, but Louella had had her heart set on it for months, so off they all went.

The guests who rode would join in the chase, and those who didn't would mingle over mimosas and bloody Marys until everyone returned for brunch.

Lil awoke early, in her yellow and lilac bedroom, to Dan's tongue in her ear. She smiled and turned in his arms. "Mmm. There's nothing more wonderful than waking up with the man you love."

Dan kissed her nose and then wrinkled his. "I don't want to wake up with any man, whether I love him or not."

She shoved him playfully in the chest. "You know what I mean."

"Yeah. Speaking of waking up next to you, we should talk. Because the last time I checked, Connecticut wasn't too close to Texas on the map."

She ran her finger along his stubbly jaw. "No, it's not. And I'm not sure what to do about that."

"Can I make a suggestion?"

Lil nodded.

"I have a program in the works. Starting next summer, I'll have anywhere from twenty to forty at-risk urban boys coming out to spend time at my place. They'll take some classes, they'll do some chores, and have some fun. They'll learn what it takes to run a working ranch."

"That's wonderful, Dan. Why? How did this come about?"

"It came about because I remember being a fourteen-year-old kid whose mother had taken off, a kid with a bad attitude and a penchant for trouble. I can relate to these boys. I can try to head them away from trouble and set them on a better course."

She kissed him. "You're such an amazing, generous person."

He snorted. "Nah. I'm just gonna be a guy with a lot of headaches. I'm not under any illusions that I won't be pulling these kids out of scrapes, you know? But what I wanted to talk to you about is this—most of them are coming from tough backgrounds and they have no idea how to conduct themselves off the basketball court or the football field.

"If they're ever going to have a chance to go to college or into the business world, they need to know how to behave and how to dress. And how to treat a lady."

"I'd love to," she said.

"You would? Really?"

"Yes. I can't think of a better use of my time."

"I'm not askin' you to leave Connecticut for good. I could spend time up there with you, too. I was kinda thinkin' that the summer and fall is nicer up there, and the winter and spring are nicer in Texas."

"Oh, you were, were you?" She laughed. "How are you going to run a ranch in Amarillo from Farmington, Connecticut?"

"I haven't figured that part out, yet. But my dad is there, and so are my cousins. How are you going to be Miss Connecticut Etiquette in Texas?"

She kissed him. "Why, I'll just be in charge of expanding Finesse's southwestern division, that's all."

"Think you can get used to cow patties?"

"For you," she said, running a hand over his chest, "I can get used to anything. As long as you take me to the opera in Dallas every once in a while."

"Opera?" Dan's head shot up from where he'd been nuzzling her breast. "That wasn't part of the bargain! I hate that fruity cat-strangling."

"Opera for cow patties. I think it's a fair trade, don't you?"

He groaned. "Okay, okay." He went back to her breasts and all was quiet except for her quickened breathing and occasional sound of pleasure. Then he raised his head again.

"Lil? Do you even own a pair of jeans?"

"Yes, believe it or not I have several pairs."

"Boots?"

"Yes, but they're Prada."

"Who?"

"Never mind."

"We'll get you some real boots."

"Do I have to wear a belt like yours, too?"

"If you really hate it that much, we'll get you a concho belt."

"Deal."

All conversation ended at that point, because Dan went south from her breasts and words just didn't seem so important any longer.

Nana Lisbeth would not have approved of her granddaughter having relations with a man while she was a guest under someone else's roof.

Nana wouldn't approve of her having unmarried relations at all. Lisbeth London had done her very best to teach Lil what was right.

Good thing this felt so very, very right.

Standing in the shower with Dan half an hour later, Lil soaped his back, not to mention other things and felt that she'd finally joined her own generation. She'd put down her tea and had tequila. She'd ditched her panty hose and worn a thong. And she'd discovered that she liked her sex hot, spicy and often!

She would always love her grandmother. But she needed to live her own life, not Nana's.

"ARE YOU READY to go?" Lil knocked on Dan's door after she'd gotten dressed.

He opened it, clasping his watch on his wrist. "Yep."

He wore not a red jacket and riding breeches, but a pair of blue jeans and his cowboy boots.

"Where are your clothes for the chase?"

"You're lookin' at 'em."

"You can't ride like that!"

"Yes, I can. I've made special arrangements." He grinned at her. "Come on, honey, let's go show these English how it's done."

She had a sinking feeling in the pit of her stomach. "Dan? What are you up to?"

"I don't know what you mean," he said, all innocence.

"I think your mother has a gun. You should keep that in mind."

He laughed. "Mama and I had a chat. You may see a change in her attitude about a lot of things."

LIL DIDN'T RIDE, which was something that Dan promised to remedy. So she was on the terrace with the other guests, sipping a mimosa, when the participants in the chase gathered in their red jackets on their glorious thoroughbreds.

She was exchanging small talk with Lovely Nigel, who'd unbent enough to tell her all about cricket, when the poor man choked, pointed and bit down so hard on his cigar that he chomped right through it.

Lil turned and was not entirely unsurprised to see the love of her life seated on a huge Appaloosa with a monumental Western saddle. He wore his jeans, a pair of leather chaps, a T-shirt, cowboy boots and a huge grin.

Lovely Nigel sputtered and coughed while Lil tried,

and failed, to hide her smile. Louella took one look and drained her bloody Mary, poking herself in the eye with the celery stalk. Then she went for another.

"Preposterous!" exclaimed one matron, as the master of ceremonies blinked at Dan.

"Obnoxious!" said a gentleman with bad teeth.

"Perfect," murmured Lil.

The master of ceremonies seemed reluctant to allow Dan to participate. He headed toward him and they exchanged words. Then a familiar figure cantered toward them, her blond curls escaping from her black hat.

Claire spoke with the MC and he blustered. She reasoned. He waffled. She reasoned some more. Finally the man threw his hands wide in a gesture of defeat.

He sounded the trumpet and the steeplechase began. Dan and all the rest of them were off. Lil closed her eyes as he flew over a huge hedge, Western saddle and all, and disappeared from sight.

If he didn't break his neck, she was going to marry him.

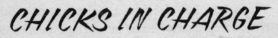

If you enjoyed what you just read,
then we've got an offer you can't resist!

Take 2 bestselling love stories FREE!

Plus get a FREE surprise gift!

Clip this page and mail it to Harlequin Reader Service®

IN U.S.A.
3010 Walden Ave.
P.O. Box 1867
Buffalo, N.Y. 14240-1867

IN CANADA
P.O. Box 609
Fort Erie, Ontario
L2A 5X3

YES! Please send me 2 free Harlequin® Blaze™ novels and my free surprise gift. After receiving them, if I don't wish to receive anymore, I can return the shipping statement marked cancel. If I don't cancel, I will receive 6 brand-new novels each month, before they're available in stores! In the U.S.A., bill me at the bargain price of $3.99 plus 25¢ shipping and handling per book and applicable sales tax, if any*. In Canada, bill me at the bargain price of $4.47 plus 25¢ shipping and handling per book and applicable taxes**. That's the complete price and a savings of at least 10% off the cover prices—what a great deal! I understand that accepting the 2 free books and gift places me under no obligation ever to buy any books. I can always return a shipment and cancel at any time. Even if I never buy another book from Harlequin, the 2 free books and gift are mine to keep forever.

151 HDN D7ZZ
351 HDN D72D

Name	(PLEASE PRINT)	
Address	Apt.#	
City	State/Prov.	Zip/Postal Code

Not valid to current Harlequin® Blaze™ subscribers.

Want to try two free books from another series?
Call 1-800-873-8635 or visit www.morefreebooks.com.

* Terms and prices subject to change without notice. Sales tax applicable in N.Y.
** Canadian residents will be charged applicable provincial taxes and GST.
  All orders subject to approval. Offer limited to one per household.
  ® and ™ are registered trademarks owned and used by the trademark owner and/or its licensee.

BLZ05   ©2005 Harlequin Enterprises Limited.

HARLEQUIN®

COMING NEXT MONTH

#219 GIVE ME FEVER Karen Anders
Red Letter Nights

When Tally Addison's brother goes missing, she knows who to turn to—gorgeous ex-cop Christian Castille. Only, when she and Christian stumble into a search for hidden treasure, she discovers she's already found hers...in him.

#220 HOT SPOT Debbi Rawlins
Do Not Disturb

She's got the sexiest man in America and Madison Tate is going to...take his photograph? In fact, she's counting on the hot picture to win a magazine cover contest that could make her career. But when Jack Logan balks at even removing his shirt, Madison knows she'll have to use a little feminine *persuasion*.... Good thing the photo shoot is at the seductive Hush hotel....

#221 ALL I WANT... Isabel Sharpe
The Wrong Bed

Krista Marlow wanted two things for Christmas—a sexy man and a lasting relationship. Well, she got the sexy man one night when she and Seth Wellington ended up in bed in the same cozy cabin. But would the relationship survive New Year's once Seth revealed his true identity?

#222 DON'T OPEN TILL CHRISTMAS Leslie Kelly

Social worker Noelle Bradenton has never believed in Santa. But when a thieving St. Nick drops cop Mark Santori at her door, Noelle has to rethink her opinion of Christmas. Because Mark is one present she'd definitely like to unwrap....

#223 GETTING IT NOW! Rhonda Nelson
Chicks in Charge

TV chef Carrie Robbins would do anything to get her show off the ground—even parade around half-dressed! But when the network hooks her up with stuffy British chef Phillip Mallory, she's ready to quit...until it becomes obvious that the oven isn't the only thing heating up....

#224 FASCINATION Samantha Hunter
The HotWires, Bk. 1

Sage Matthews's fascination with computer hacking got her into deep trouble. Just ask FBI agent Ian Chandler, who arrested the fiery redhead—and has been watching her every sexy move since. Now she's ready for a fresh start, but Ian's fascination with her is about to bring him more trouble than he ever imagined.

www.eHarlequin.com

HBCNM1105